HER ETERNAL WARRIOR

OMEGA SKY
BOOK 7

CAITLYN O'LEARY

© Copyright 2024 Caitlyn O'Leary
All rights reserved.
All cover art and logo © Copyright 2024
By Passionately Kind Publishing Inc.
Cover by Lori Jackson Design
Cover by Lori Jackson Design
Edited by Sally Keller
Content Edited by Trenda Lundin
Technical Editor, Abha Datwani

All rights reserved. No part of this book may be reproduced in any form or by any electronic or mechanical means, including information storage and retrieval systems—except in the case of brief quotations embodied in critical articles or reviews—without permission in writing from the author.

This book is a work of fiction. The names, characters, and places portrayed in this book are entirely products of the author's imagination or used fictitiously. Any resemblance to actual events, locales or persons, living or dead, is entirely coincidental and not intended by the author.

The unauthorized reproduction or distribution of this copyrighted work is illegal. Criminal copyright infringement, including infringement without monetary gain, is investigated by the FBI and is punishable by up to five years in federal prison and a fine of $250,000.

If you find any eBooks being sold or shared illegally, please contact the author at Caitlyn@CaitlynOLeary.com.

I couldn't have written this book without the help of Abha Datwani. Her knowledge of South Asia and the South Asian culture was invaluable. Personally, Abha is someone I have come to know and respect over the years, and it was a delight to finally get to work with her in such an in-depth manner. I have learned a lot from her, and I really appreciate her willingness to help me.

SYNOPSIS

She Needed a Hero

Tied up, tossed in a truck, and locked in a muddy shack, Jenny Rivers is sure she is going to die, because if her captors don't kill her, her injuries probably will.

Navy SEAL Braxton Walker's job is brutal, but he thrives on it. Parachuting into Bangladesh to rescue a woman is all in a day's work.

Determined to keep her alive, as mercenaries are on their trail, his only thought is to keep Jenny safe. But has he finally found something beyond his capabilities?

This is an action, adventure, romantic, stand-alone novel.

PROLOGUE

They were fighting again. They were always fighting these days. Brax stepped over his baseball bat to get to his desk. He wanted his headphones.

"I'm leaving."

"The hell you are! Your daughter needs you!"

Brax stopped mid-stride.

"Lou, you don't understand. I can't handle it. It's too much."

"You can't handle it? You can't handle it? CiCi is lying in a hospital bed, and you say you can't handle it? I can't effing believe you."

Brax had never heard his dad sound so angry. Had his mom really said she was leaving? That couldn't be right. Not with CiCi so sick.

"This is the third time she's been in the hospital. Every time they say she's going to get better, and then she relapses. I keep having to put my life on hold. I can't be expected to live like this."

"Our daughter's only seven years old. Please, Candy,

you can't do this. She needs you. She needs her mother."

Now his dad didn't sound angry. He sounded like he was begging. Like when Kenny Renfrew begged the coach for a third chance and started crying.

"No, Lou, I'm already packed."

"But tomorrow she starts another round of treatments," his dad said. Was he going to cry?

"I'm just taking the car, my clothes and what's in the checking account. I'm not touching our savings. You'll be fine."

"How can you say that? How? How am I expected to tell CiCi that her mother left?"

"You'll think of something. I don't know. Tell her my mother had an accident, and I needed to be with her."

"You hate your mother. We haven't seen her in four years. What the hell am I going to tell Brax?" Now he was starting to sound mad again.

Brax strained to hear them, but they weren't talking. Finally his mother said something. "I'll go talk to him. You might not understand what I'm doing, but my son will. He knows what I'm going through. He's seen my pain. He's seen my sacrifice."

"Bullshit, Candy. Brax will be madder than me."

"You've never understood the special bond between a mother and her son. Braxton will understand."

Brax heard his parents' door open. He could hear his mother's heels clicking on the hardwood floor. They stopped outside his door. His mother knocked softly.

"Braxton, honey, Mom needs to talk to you. Can I come in?"

He went over to the door and opened it. His mom was dressed nice, in a skirt and sweater with necklaces. Her hair was all poofed and curled, too. Like the old times when she would go out with her friends from work. Or when she went out with Sally or Kathy. If he hadn't heard the fight he would have thought it was just another night out, like normal.

His mom came into his room and sat on the side of his bed. He was supposed to sit beside her, for one of their talks, like normal. He didn't. He sat in his desk chair and turned it around so he could watch her.

"I guess you're too old for mother-and-son talks on the side of the bed, like we used to have, huh?" She gave him her sad face. He knew he was supposed to go sit next to her now, but he didn't. Dad was right. He was mad.

"What do you want to talk about?" Maybe he could talk her out of leaving. Dad was right about another thing too; CiCi needed her.

His mom leaned forward, her elbows on her knees. "You've caught me crying sometimes, haven't you?"

He nodded.

"The last two years have been really hard with your sister in and out of the hospital," she whispered.

"Yeah, for all of us," he said clearly. "But mostly for CiCi." He saw his mother wince.

"Your sister has had a lot of support and attention. The nurses and doctors have been with her constantly. Then we have been at her bedside all the time. I even quit my job when CiCi was five years old when she relapsed a second time..."

Brax nodded.

"You know," she prodded.

"Yes, Mom, I know."

"Come here, and sit next to your mom." Brax reluctantly got up and sat next to her, and she put her arm around him. "I loved my job. I was going to *be* someone."

Brax had heard her say that more times than he could count. She talked all the time about the promotion she was going to get and having to give up her dreams at the magazine because CiCi kept getting sick. But now was different.

"Mom, maybe you can do both. I'm older. I can help." Brax was desperate. "I'm eleven. Maybe you can go back to your old job, and Dad and me could be the ones to visit CiCi all the time. You can just see her on weekends. How about that?"

Please let her say yes.

She squeezed him tight, and he smelled the perfume she was wearing. It didn't smell the same as always. All the other times it smelled sweet and nice, this time it smelled almost sour.

"Braxton, you have always been my good little man. You've always been on my side, no matter what. That's why I love you so much."

"And CiCi, you love CiCi too, right?"

"Of course I love CiCi. But it's you who I've always relied on to understand me. To believe in me. And you have, Braxton. You have." She brushed back a lock of his brown hair. "I've always believed in your dreams, and you've always believed in mine."

Suddenly, he didn't want to become an astronaut. Not if his dream would take him away from his sister. Not if his dream would make him go away from his family.

"But why do you have to leave?"

His mom winced. "You heard your dad and me talking?"

Brax nodded. "Can't you just call up your old boss and get your old job back?" he pleaded.

"No, I decided it was time I moved on to a bigger and brighter future. I applied for a job in New York. They liked my ideas and I've been hired. I'm going to be a Social Media Intern for three months, and then I will be a full-time Social Media Assistant. This magazine is read by over a million people!"

She squeezed Brax so hard he could hardly breathe. "Brax, that's my first step to becoming the Senior Fashion Editor. *Me*, a girl from Iowa! Can you imagine that?" She bounced on the bed.

He shook his head. He didn't know what she was talking about. All he heard was that she was leaving them. Leaving CiCi. His sister had the biggest brown eyes, and she hardly ever cried. Not even when they used those big needles on her. Dad told him that the cancer hurt her all the time, but CiCi always tried to smile when Brax was in the room. So Brax smiled. He saved his tears for when he was home.

"Mom, you can't leave. It's not right."

His mom pulled her arm away and looked at him. "I thought you would understand."

"I don't understand. I don't understand how you would do something that would make CiCi so sad."

She stood up.

"She's strong. She'll be okay."

Brax shot up off his bed, his arms stiff by his sides, his fists clenched. "You're wrong. She's not strong. She just tries to be to make us feel better. You're supposed to be the one to help her. You're supposed to hold her. It's the right thing to do."

His mom knelt down in front of him. "One day you'll understand. The right thing for me to do is follow my own dreams."

He looked her dead in the eye. "No, Mom, I. Will. Never. Understand."

He sucked in a deep breath so he wouldn't cry or yell.

"Not ever."

1

"Jenny, why are two policemen outside your house?" Ahmed Banik asked. She could hear both concern and fright in his voice. His sisters sitting in the back seat, Sabina and Sonia, murmured to each other. Jenny and Sabina worked together at New Era Cyber Tech in Dhaka. Currently, Jenny was the highest-ranking executive for the company in country.

Jenny peered out the passenger side window and frowned. The two men were in teal-blue police uniforms, and they stood in front of the house that she'd been renting for the last two years while she worked in Bangladesh.

"They probably want to ask Jenny another round of questions," Sabina answered her brother's question for Jenny. What Sabina said was probably true, but it still sent a frisson of discomfort up Jenny's spine to see the police at her home.

She'd heard the horror stories about what some of the police had perpetrated in the last year, and it had made her blood run cold. Granted, it was just a few outliers, but most people thought they were doing the bidding of the Awani League. They were the government in charge at the moment.

Stop it! You're overreacting, Rivers!

Jenny took a deep breath and worked to keep her breathing at a comfortable rate.

I am not scared. I am not scared.

Jenny concentrated on the fact that her company had assured every single employee from the US—CEO and executives multiple times—that they were completely safe in Bangladesh, despite the unrest.

"Maybe we should just turn around and go to our parents' house," Ahmed suggested. "We'll pretend we're still hiking in Sreemangal."

"If I keep them waiting, it'll only make things worse," Jenny said. "You head on home. I'll handle things."

"No. It's better if we both go," Sabina protested. "We both work for NECT. Remember, the rule is to stick together."

"I'm the highest-ranking NECT employee here in Bangladesh since Mr. Roberts and Mrs. Tyree left last week. I need to handle this. You stay with your brother and sister."

Jenny opened the car door and stepped out onto the small drive that led up to her bungalow. The two men stood straighter, their rifles pointing up behind them.

"How can I help you?" Jenny asked.

"You are Jennifer Rivers," the first officer asked. "You work for New Tera Tech."

"New Era Cyber Tech," Jenny corrected.

The young man's mouth twisted and his brow furled. "That's what I said. New Era Tech Cyber," he spit out. "We have questions for you. You need to come with us."

The other police officers who had come to her office to talk to her, had the name of the company. NECT backed up many of the servers and websites for various competing political coalitions and the universities that were currently protesting.

NECT's international stance had been and always would be apolitical. As someone who had a master's degree in public relations, Jenny understood this, and had always felt comfortable explaining her company's position. She'd been working in public relations for eight years. This was not her first rodeo.

"You need to come with us," the second officer said. "Now." He looked over her shoulder, then she turned and saw that Ahmed had gotten out of the car and was leaning against it with his arms crossed.

"Tell your boyfriend to get back in the car," the younger, surly officer demanded.

"He's not my boyfriend and I'm not getting in your car. Now tell me what you want."

"Our supervisor needs to ask you a few questions," the older officer, who spoke better English, said.

Now that Jenny was over the surprise of these men showing up at her house, she was noticing things. Their shoes were wrong. They were wearing two different kinds of boots. The police had a specific type of boot—black with a rounded toe—and one of the men had brown boots on. Also, the young man, besides having horrible sweat stains on his teal uniform, was missing a button. Jenny had never seen such a thing. Police officers took pride in their uniforms.

The young man grabbed her upper arm. "Let's go."

"Let me go," she shouted.

"Let her go," the sisters yelled from the car.

Jenny was hurled to the ground as the young officer let go of her when Ahmed's shoulder hit the young man's stomach. It was like Ahmed played tackle for the Cincinnati Bengals football team.

"No," Jenny screamed. Attacking a member of the Bangladeshi was a terrible offense.

"Ahmed, no!" Sonia or Sabina yelled from the car.

Jenny heard the car door opening. She pushed herself up from the ground and pointed at Sonia, the younger sister. "Stay there. You'll only make things worse."

The older officer was helping up the younger officer, while keeping his rifle pointed at Ahmed.

"He was hurting her. Look at her arm. It's going to bruise." Ahmed pleaded his case. The man didn't turn to look at Jenny. He kept his rifle trained on Ahmed.

"Crawl to the stairs. Over there," the older officer said. He motioned to Jenny's front porch.

"What are you waiting for?" The younger man demanded to know. "Kill him. Kill him now. Rakib said no witnesses."

The senior officer casually twirled his rifle and used the butt of it to smash it into the young officer's face. Jenny could swear she heard his nose break. The older man turned back to Ahmed. "Crawl faster," he said as he turned the rifle back on him. He waited until Ahmed was at the stairs.

"Listen here, you piece of dog shit," The older man turned to the young man who was bleeding out his nose. "Don't use our leader's name again, or I'll shoot you. Next, we do want witnesses. We're wearing the Bangladeshi Police force uniforms. That poor bastard," he pointed to Ahmed. "And the women in the car would have testified that the police took her. It would have been perfect. Now it will be just the women."

"Are you taking orders from the Awani League government?" Jenny whispered her question.

The older man smiled while the young man went over to Ahmed and ripped his shirt off him in order to use it to staunch the bleeding from his broken nose.

"Miss Rivers, before your adventure is done, you'll wish we were the Awani League. Alas, we're old-fashioned. We want money. Small change. Two billion *takas*. Today, that's a little less than twenty million dollars. Your company makes that much in four hours each day. Surely, they can pay that for you?"

Jenny shivered. She knew that New Era Cyber Tech had kidnapping and ransom insurance, but they had assured her they had never once had to use it. What's more, India was one of America's allies. America did business with India all the time, and Bangladesh should be considered a sister country to India. But she knew they were very different nations, and had voiced her concerns. She was all but laughed off. The more

Jenny had talked to the Banik brother and sisters, the more concerned she became.

"I know how much two billion *takas*, is," Jenny said calmly. She wanted them to know that she'd taken the time to learn about Bangladesh as she tried to soothe them.

The older man laughed. "You're funny. Don't think you can talk your way out of this."

"I don't." She bowed her head. "Please don't hurt them."

"If you come easily, there will be no need," the older man said.

"The man needs to die. He's heard too much," the young hot head shouted.

"And whose fault is that?"

"Please," Jenny begged. "I will do what you say."

"Don't worry, if you come calmly, no one will die. Bring the truck." The older officer motioned to his minion. The young man reluctantly trotted around the side of Jenny's house, and she soon heard the roar of a truck coming to life.

When it drove to the front, she shuddered. It was a box truck, with just two seats in front. Obviously, she was going to have to go in the back. She couldn't read the writing on the side of the truck, but the logo was clear. It was a butcher shop.

Please let it be empty.

"Tie her up."

The young man grinned as he yanked her arms behind her back and tied them together at her elbows. He tied them tight. Then he started at her wrists. She did what she remembered from some TV show or another and kept her wrists a little bit apart so she would have wiggle room.

Yeah, like that's going to make a difference.

The rope was coarse and scratchy. It hurt already.

"Don't forget her ankles," the older one pointed out.

"Then I'll have to carry her," the other kidnapper whined.

"There is definitely something wrong with your generation. Quit your complaining, tie her up and carry her to the truck," the other man ground out.

At least the rope was tied over her boots.

The angry young man shoved his shoulder into her stomach, then lifted her up and soon she was hanging upside down over his shoulder.

She heard a shot, then she heard Sabina and Sonia screaming.

Oh God, he shot Ahmed!

She heard the truck's door clang open, then the young man tossed her upward. Her forehead cracked against metal and her nose and mouth filled with liquid covering the floor. She inhaled in shock and choked on it. It was cold, but the coppery taste was foul.

Blood!

She jerked up her head as best she could and tried to scream, but the blood in her lungs made her cough.

"Get me out of here. Let me out," she begged as she spit blood out of her mouth.

"Shut up. Figure out a way to roll over, and you'll be fine."

Jenny looked over at the young officer and saw his maniacal pleasure. He laughed.

"Enjoy your time. Just wait until we start driving over rocks, then you'll really have fun."

Jenny had a moment to look around and saw that there was no meat hanging from the hooks, but the notched floor of the truck had blood an inch deep in each of the runnels, and her mouth had landed in one of them. Then the door clanged shut and her entire world went black.

Without being able to see anything, she could hear the blood sloshing around, and smell and taste the copper in the air.

I'm in hell.

2

"Oh God, you really are a teenager, aren't you?" Brax looked up at the sky for any kind of an answer. "Why me? She was so much fun and good up until now."

He crouched down and looked over at Faith. "Come on, girl. Come." He patted his knees. Faith started to run toward him and Brax sighed in relief. Then she ran past him and picked up the knotted rope ten feet behind him. She brought it back to him and dropped it in front of Brax. His puppy looked up expectantly.

"That's fetch, Faith. Come on, for the last four months you've known the difference between fetch and come. What in the hell is up with you?"

She looked at him, then turned her head and literally gave him the side-eye. She ran back to her seesaw and started trying to balance on it. Every time she slid down one side, she'd climb up and try again. It was clear she was having a blast.

Yep, it was playtime, not training time. Typical teenager. She had no use for school.

Dammit. At this rate he was going to have to send her to military school. Brax huffed out a laugh.

BUD/S for teenage dogs. That would be something. At least she wasn't into clothes and make-up. "Come on, girl. We've got to go. Time to go visit Hercules."

Brax watched as Faith got off the see-saw in a shot and beat him to the back door of his recently purchased house. "So, was it me saying 'come' or me saying 'Hercules'?"

Woof

"Come?"

Faith stared at Brax.

"Hercules?"

Woof

"So, you're boy crazy. Figures."

"Down."

Brax watched in amazement as both black Russian Terrier pups plunked their asses on Mateo and Lainey's tiled floor. Lainey hadn't even offered Faith a treat, and she was calmly sitting, waiting for Lainey's next command.

What the fuck?

"Good puppies," Lainey crooned.

"Go lay down." She pointed to the large doggie bed that took up a corner of her and Mateo's living room. They both got up and trotted over to the bed where

Xena rested. She looked up at them and gave a welcoming yip but she didn't move. Faith and Hercules lay down on either side of her, and all three were soon fast asleep.

"How in the hell do you do that?" Brax demanded to know.

"That's what I keep asking," Mateo said as he gave Brax the smoothie he'd just made.

"Thanks." Brax smiled.

"Do you want one?" Mateo asked Lainey.

"Does it have kale in it?"

"Absolutely." Mateo grinned.

"Then absolutely not."

"You didn't answer the question. How did you get Faith to obey you? She's not listening to any command I give her. Two months ago she had them all down pat. I've read up on all of this and apparently she's a teenager now, but that can't be right."

Lainey laughed as she slid past him to go into the now vacant kitchen. Mateo came to stand beside Brax on the other side of the kitchen island, where they both watched the three sleeping dogs.

"Hercules pulls that same shit with me," Mateo admitted. "But he's right back to normal when Lainey tells him what to do. Granted, she uses a different voice. She calls it her mom voice."

"So stuck-up and bitchy?" Brax asked right before he took another sip of his smoothie. Everybody on his and Mateo's SEAL team knew that Lainey's mother had belittled her for years, and they all felt very protective of Lainey.

"No, Brax," Lainey sighed. "It's my no-nonsense voice. Deep down, Mateo thinks the whole thing is kind of funny, and I bet you do too."

"Lainey, that's not the deal. I'm really frustrated. I'm thinking about enrolling her into a doggie training program for a couple of weeks, but that's admitting defeat. I should be able to handle this on my own. So, tell me what this *mom voice* of yours is all about."

"What different voices do you use with her?" Lainey asked.

"Huh?"

"Voices? Do you yell at her?"

"Nope. I know better than that. I try to stay calm, but sometimes she frustrates the hell out of me and I think she catches on."

"She probably does."

"Does Hercules catch on with me?" Mateo asked.

"Yep," Lainey answered.

"Why didn't you tell me?"

"You told me that I was the one who was in charge of training him, remember?"

Mateo squeezed the back of his neck as he looked at his fiancée. "I did, didn't I?"

She nodded, with a sparkle in her eye.

"Okay, teach us both," Mateo half requested and half demanded.

"Oh, so now you want to learn," she teased.

"Damn right I do. No telling where else that might come in handy."

Lainey grinned. "Okay, here's the deal. You both need to use different tones of voice so the dogs know what you're trying to convey. They know your voice when you want to play, since you two *always* want to play."

"You got that right," Mateo winked.

"Pay attention," Brax ordered his friend. "I want to understand this. Go ahead, Lainey."

"Let's go out to the backyard where they can't hear us as well."

They all trooped out to the big backyard and sat down at the picnic table.

"You need to have a voice that they can associate with positive reinforcement. When we're still in a training phase give them a treat. If they've done really well, give them a better treat."

"Makes sense," Brax nodded. "What else?"

"Then there's time-outs."

"Like a kid?" Mateo asked.

"Exactly. First, if they're acting out, doing things like misbehaving, jumping, or barking, just turn around and ignore it. Because they're trying to get your attention through negative behavior. When they realize it can't work, they should stop what they're doing. If that isn't working, then they need a brief time-out. Send them to a corner. Use a calm, firm voice. This voice is one you're going to use again and again. After Faith or Hercules have calmed down, you can invite them to come out again."

Brax really liked what he was hearing. He looked over at his friend, and he could see that Mateo was really into all the information that Lainey was giving him, too.

"Often all you need to do is redirect their energy toward a positive activity like playing with a toy, or practicing a command they know, like sit or heel."

"Should you do that before putting them in time out?" Mateo asked.

"Judge their behavior and decide," Lainey explained. "You're the boss."

"Just like a child?" Brax asked in a tentative voice.

"I wouldn't know. I just read stuff off the internet and went into an on-line chat group. One man in there definitely said it was like handling his teenagers." Lainey laughed.

"What else?" Mateo asked.

"Try to always keep it fun. Distraction is a great tool. If they're doing something they shouldn't, like chewing on your shoe like Hercules did."

"Yeah, the bastard only stopped when you tempted him outside with the frisbee. I should have thought of that."

"The website said the key is to always praise good behavior. End on a high note. Try to stay away from saying things like 'bad dog.' We're supposed to always stay calm."

Brax looked over at Mateo and snorted.

"Hey, I can do calm like a motherfucker."

"Sure you can." Brax smiled.

"I can."

Lainey went over to her fiancé, wrapped her arm around his waist, and slid her hand up his chest. "Yes, you can. You've been calm with me when I've been out of sorts."

Mateo smiled.

"See how she ends on a positive note with you?" Brax laughed.

"You're just jealous," Mateo smirked.

"And the last thing I learned is that you need to increase mental and physical exercise so your pups can burn off all that energy they have. Make sure they have mental and physical stimuli to keep them entertained. It'll help reduce misbehavior."

"See, I've got it all kinds of good," Mateo crooned.

"Before I have to witness any physical stimulus between the two of you, I'm taking my dog and we're out of here." They went back inside and Brax got Faith's leash. "Come on, girl, we're going for a ride."

Faith's ears perked up, and she hustled on over to him.

"Yep, a car ride. We're going to go see your aunt CiCi. What do you think about that?"

Woof.

Woof.

CiCi flung open the door.

"Brax!"

His baby sister threw herself into his arms. She weighed practically nothing, and he didn't even have to take a step backward. Feeling the strength of her hug was the sweetest feeling in the world.

"CiCi, you look beautiful."

"Bullshit." She smiled as she looked up at him. "I

look like a woman who has been cleaning house for the last four hours. Hardly my best look." She peeked around him and squealed.

"You brought Faith." His sister struggled to get out of his arms, but Brax held on.

"Oh, no you don't. Faith is a handful these days, I'll bring her in so you can play. Where's dad? Why isn't he helping you clean?"

"We're past the point of me needing help to clean a toilet. I've been given the all clear. I'm gaining weight, and, and, and... Guess who's been lifting weights? Guess who has actually discovered the joy of jogging? Not fast mind you, but still, I'm jogging."

Her grin was incandescent.

"Are you sure you're not confusing jogging with speed walking? You know, where you waddle? They do it in the malls in the morning."

CiCi hit him in the chest. Harder than he anticipated. It made him happy.

"I'm sure. I'm not a waddler."

"Is waddler a word?"

"Just shut the hell up and get Faith. I want to play with her. You, I'm not so sure about."

"Do you have anything to eat? I'm hungry."

"When aren't you? Hurry and get your butt inside."

"And when did you develop such a potty mouth?" Brax threw the question over his shoulder as he headed for the driveway.

"Every bad word I use, I've learned from you," she yelled after him.

Brax grunted.

He let Faith out of the truck, and before he could get a leash on her, she was bounding her way up to the door to greet CiCi. The one good thing was that she stopped and waited to be petted. She always went in gentle with his little sister. At least she remembered something. Brax sighed. He followed his two girls into his dad's house. He could smell lemon wax, but there was something else. Was that chocolate?

"Did you know I was coming?"

"It's the weekend. I had a good idea." CiCi grinned at him as she led him into the sparkling kitchen. He saw the chocolate cake on the covered cake stand. There wasn't even a piece taken out of it. He'd be the first person to get a slice.

"Do you have—"

"Of course I have cherry sauce to go with it," she said with an indulgent smile.

She turned to the refrigerator as Brax took the top off the glass plate and inhaled.

"I'm forever in Mrs. Baumgartner's debt for teaching you how to cook."

"I miss her," CiCi said with a sad smile. "She was good to all of us."

Brax nodded. He watched as his sister cut him a large slice, then drizzled cherry sauce on top. She cut a much smaller slice for herself, but it was still much bigger than it used to be, and that warmed his heart. That experimental treatment had been the best thing that had ever happened to their family.

"Where's Dad?" Brax asked after he swallowed two bites of heaven.

"He's with Jerry and John. They're playing pool."

"Oh yeah, he was pretty pissed he lost two dollars the last time they played," Brax remembered.

"That was three weekends ago. Now he's up four dollars."

"Still can't buy a mocha."

"Like he'd ever step foot in a fancy coffee shop," CiCi countered.

They both laughed. The idea of Henry Walker buying anything other than a black coffee at some diner or gas station was unthinkable.

"I'm glad you stopped by. I wanted to talk to you about something."

Brax didn't like hearing the hesitation in his sister's voice. Anything other than happy and positive always scared him. It reminded him too much of all those times she'd been in and out of hospitals. Those times when he and his dad were holding out for the next miracle.

"Stop it." CiCi hit him on his chest, and he grabbed her hand.

"Tell me."

"Seriously, stop it. I can't stand it when you immediately go to the dark side. That's why I'm coming to you first. Dad is even worse. I need to be able to have a normal conversation with you without the specter of my death hanging over us. I'm good. I'm well. The doctors all think that the cancer isn't coming back. Now let's all move on."

He wished he heard just exasperation in his sister's voice. But underneath it, he could hear her pleading to be treated normally. Who could blame her? Who in the world could fucking blame her? She'd been living life on the edge for as long as he could remember. Goddamn right it was time for him to be treating her normally.

"Hit me with it." He grinned.

"You mean it?"

"Absolutely. Anything you want to talk about, aside from feminine products, I'm up for."

CiCi giggled. "How about my sex life?"

"Shit, Dad hasn't had the 'talk' with you? I suppose if you need to know what's what, I can tell you what Ryker was like before meeting Amy and you'll know that you need to stay a virgin until you get married at the ripe old age of forty-five."

CiCi lifted an eyebrow. "What makes you think I'm still a virgin?"

Brax stopped mid-thought.

What?

"Well, of course you're a virgin. I mean—"

"Yes?"

He stared at his baby sister.

"Ummm. What did you want to talk about?" he asked cautiously.

"I want to move out. I've sent in my application to Virginia Peninsula Community College in Hampton and I've found the cutest little place to rent. This older couple has converted their old carriage garage into an apartment. The rent isn't all that much because I'll be looking in on them some of the time."

"College and caretaking?" He frowned.

"Brax!"

He held out his palms face up. "Sorry. It just seems like a lot to take on for anybody, that's all."

"It's a really easy job, and it means the rent is hardly anything."

"CiCi, you've only been out of the hospital for a couple of months," he protested.

"I've been out of the hospital for over a year," she sighed. "You sound just like Dad. If I don't get accepted, I still want to move out. It's time. The Vickers said they would hold the place for me, and in the meantime, I would continue to build up my endurance. The jogging and weight training have been really helping, and I'm going to continue that."

He looked down at the fierce little warrior in front of him. How had she turned out to be such a fighter when she'd been so sick and abandoned? She was more than a miracle.

"What can I do to help?" he asked.

"Be here when I break the news to Dad."

"You've got it."

3

Jenny didn't know how long it had taken her to roll to the side of the truck and prop herself up so that she wasn't wallowing in sticky blood.

Too long.

She'd spit so much, she didn't think she'd ever be able to pee again. Maybe, possibly, she wouldn't end up with the world's worst disease. Just thinking about it made her try to spit some more, but it was no use. She'd already tried to grab hold of her shirt collar with her mouth, but her hands were tied too tightly behind her back to allow her to reach forward.

"I'm fucked."

"I'm so fucked."

Thankfully, she'd found one of the wheel wells to brace herself against, but damn near every time the truck ran over another boulder she cracked her head against the side of the truck. At least she wouldn't fall over.

Now she was going to suffer from a brain bleed along with some heretofore unheard of infectious, parasitic disease. She'd be written up in medical journals around the world.

Yeah, if they ever find my corpse.

"Snap out of it! You've faced worse challenges than this! Okay, maybe a backhand or punch from dear old Dad wasn't worse than this but still. You survived."

She shivered. *Really?*

"How in the hell can I be shivering in Bangladesh during the hot and sticky monsoon season?"

Bang.

Her head crashed against metal again and Jenny saw stars. She thought she might have actually passed out for a moment. She took a deep breath.

Dammit!

She'd breathed through her nose.

Gah! I'm going to throw-up. The stench.

For a moment she wanted to cry as she forced herself to take three steady breaths through her mouth.

No crying. She could breathe. She was alive.

Ahmed. How could she have forgotten Ahmed? They'd shot him.

But she'd only heard the one shot before they'd gotten in the truck. That meant that Sabina and Sonia were safe. They would be going for help. They'd tell people what had happened. Or would they?

How could they possibly go to the police and say they saw men in police uniforms shoot their brother and kidnap their co-worker? Who would possibly believe them? What's more, if they ended up talking to police who were being bribed by the Awami League, wouldn't they be targeted? They hadn't heard the men say that they were actually kidnappers, only Ahmed had heard that.

This time when her head hit against the side of the truck, she wasn't sure if it was because the truck went over something, or she was hitting her head against the side in frustration.

Does it really matter?

Shifting again, her elbows found an empty spot between the wheel well and the side of the truck, and she sighed with relief. Jenny tried to think of something good. Anything good. Closing her eyes, she started to take slow, deep breaths through her mouth. In, then out.

Soon she wasn't breathing in the scent of warm copper.

She imagined herself at the top of Duke's Run, in Breckenridge.

She savors the cold air as she sucks it in. Jenny crouches down. She looks, and her skis are in perfect position, and her heart starts racing.

The slope stretches out before her, steep and demanding. She feels a tremor of excitement and trepidation run through her body.

It's go time.

Her poles dig into the packed snow and she starts to gain momentum. Her breath comes in quick bursts, and she grins as she sees trees streaking by her. She feels a sense of flow, a rhythm, as she twists and turns around the obstacles in her way.

I've got this.

She's in total control, her speed increases and her heart pounds as she flies. It's her and the mountain.

Together.

She's not there to conquer the mountain, she's there to connect with it. The wind whips against her cheeks. She relishes the purity of skiing, it was just her.

Her body.

Her mind.

Concentrating on nothing else but the cold air, the taste of pine and her ability to navigate every twist and turn.

She nears the bottom and begins to slow. She feels the burn in both legs as she presses against the hard-packed snow. She tries to stay upright despite the pain. Her knees absorb every dip and bump. She slips in the watery snow and her head hits the metal wheel well.

"No!" she wails. Her daydream melts away.

Jenny clenches her hands into fists, doing everything in her power to stay upright and push against the truck bed so that she can get back into an upright position.

Who was that moaning?

"Hello?"

Fuck, that's me.

"Shut up, Rivers. There's no crying when you're kidnapped, remember?"

"We were just brought in," Lieutenant Kostya Barona, of the SEAL Team Omega Sky said as his second-in-command, Gideon Smith, moved to the next picture.

Brax looked up at the screen and saw a photograph of a woman who was wearing no makeup. She was holding a staff in one hand, and she was wearing a backpack. Her hair was in one of those messy buns that so many women sported these days, but some strands had gotten loose and trailed halfway down her chest.

"This is Jenny Rivers. Two weeks ago, she went missing after hiking with a co-worker, Sabina Banik, along with Sabina's brother and sister, Ahmed and Sonia, in the Sreemangal National Park in Bangladesh. The brother was shot and killed outside Ms. Rivers' home. He wasn't found until four days after the hike took place."

"When was he killed?" Brax asked.

"The authorities in Bangladesh estimate four days prior. That would be consistent with when Ms. Rivers went missing, and the hike ended."

"Was it a group hike?" Jase asked.

Kostya nodded. "A group of ten. They talked to some of the other members of the hike, and they said the Baniks were going to drop Jenny off first since she lived in a suburb of Dhaka, and then they would proceed home to their parents' house in the city. This hike was on a Saturday, and Ms. Rivers missed work on the following Monday without calling in."

"What about the sisters?"

"They insist they left Ms. Rivers and their brother off at her house safely."

"That seems suspicious. Even if there was something going on between the brother and Ms. Rivers, she would not flaunt it in front of one of her co-workers. Even if she was his sister. As a matter of fact, that would make it even worse," Brax pointed out.

"Nah. If the Baniks lived in the capital of Bangladesh, they probably had more lax attitudes about that sort of thing," Ryker McQueen said easily.

"No, Brax is right," Gideon said as he looked up from his computer. He was the one operating the slide show. "It's not just the fact that Jenny wouldn't want her co-worker to know. A brother would never want his sisters to know about his sex life. That kind of thing is still kept hidden."

"If that's true, then their brother was killed in front of them," Brax breathed out what they were all thinking. "Why wouldn't they go to the authorities?"

"We've got to assume whoever shot the brother, took Ms. Rivers," Gideon said.

"Is there a reason?" Ryker asked.

"Nobody knows anything for sure at this point. Currently, the two sisters are being detained at the American Embassy to be questioned again, to see if they will tell us what really happened that day," Kostya said.

"Until then, are we just in a holding pattern?" Brax asked.

"Yes. I was advised about this today. The powers that be didn't think I needed to brief you on this."

"But you have a feeling, right?" Brax asked.

Kostya nodded.

"She is in charge of public relations for New Era Cyber Tech. Before she disappeared, she was the highest-ranking person for the company in Bangladesh."

"Someone in public affairs?" Linc asked. "That sounds fishy." Linc's wife was a translator who worked all over the world. Not just for the US Government, but also for big companies. Brax would bet that he had been picking up stuff about how big companies worked.

"It *is* fishy," Gideon nodded. "Just before she disappeared, the true executives for the Bangladeshi arm of the corporation had been pulled out, then the police came in and questioned Jenny at the office twice. This isn't just fishy, it's a bucket of three-day-old dead fish."

"Why are the higher ups holding off on us going in?" Brax asked.

"Because her company has sent in their K&R team."

"Please don't say they've hired a subsidiary of Kraken," Jase begged.

"Nope," Kostya assured him. "The CIA has shut down every tentacle of that hydra. There is no way that some unwitting person will ever hire them again."

"Yeah, we only have to worry about Lloyd Hicks," Jase growled.

"The CIA and Interpol are on the lookout for him. They'll find him," Kostya assured his men.

Brax and Mateo exchanged a look. After what had

happened almost a year ago, they were never going to believe they were safe until Ephram Brady's baby brother Lloyd, was captured, or better yet, killed.

"So, get your go-bags ready, and stay close to home."

Everybody nodded. If Kostya had a feeling, you could take it to the bank.

4

"Are you sure this is a good idea?" Brax murmured his question to Mateo.

"Positive. Hell, Faith will probably come out of this a better-trained pup."

Well, when he puts it that way...

He and Matteo were both drinking sodas as they watched Lainey playing with Hercules, Faith, and Lainey's rescue pup, Xena. Xena had only three legs, but she kept up. As a matter of fact, she would yip at Faith and Hercules when they were too slow to follow a command.

"Did you see that?" Mateo pointed at Xena. "That dog was afraid of her own shadow when I first met her. Ever since she attacked Ivan when he was beating Lainey, she's been fearless."

Brax could still hear the anger and anguish in his friend's voice when he thought about Lainey's captivity. He wondered if Mateo would ever be over it.

Looking out the sliding glass door, Brax would bet

his bottom dollar that Lainey was over it. Seeing how she looked at Mateo, like he was her hero and protector? Well, there was something damn special about it. Too bad that wasn't going to happen for him. Lainey and the other women of the Omega Sky men were freaking unicorns.

An image of his mother popped into his mind. Yep, Mateo and the rest had definitely hit the winning lotteries.

"Whatcha thinking?" Mateo asked as he took another sip of his soda.

"About the upcoming mission. Bangladesh. Never been there, have you?"

Mateo shook his head. "But remember the mission in Nepal? That should kind of count, right?"

Brax shrugged, then grinned.

"What?"

"We should take some R&R and head over to Italy. Hit Val Bodengo for some canyoning. I've been reading up on it."

Mateo tipped his chin toward Lainey. "If I went to Italy, it would be somewhere that Lainey and I could both enjoy. She wouldn't be happy waiting around for me to traverse a cave."

"Hey. Bite your tongue. It's a lot more than going caving. They rank Val Bodengo as one of the most difficult places to go canyoning. We'd have to be sharp."

Brax was really getting into the idea. It was stupid to do something as dangerous as canyoning on your own, and he didn't want to go with someone he didn't know, so Mateo would be perfect. They'd already done it a couple of times before.

"Sorry. Not going to happen. I'm fine risking my life for my job, but no more extreme sports for me. You can cross me off your list. I'm spending my downtime with Lainey, and I want to make sure I do everything I can to come home to her safe, whole and alive. You know what I mean."

Brax nodded. "I'm hearing you."

"Did you see that?" Mateo was pointing and laughing. "Both of them plunked their asses down at the same time. Lainey's winning."

"Winning?"

"What else would you call it? She's now the alpha." Mateo chuckled.

THE CALL CAME AT OH-TWO-HUNDRED. Brax grabbed his phone as he rolled out of bed.

"Yeah?"

"It's go-time," Gideon said.

"Bangladesh?"

"Yep."

"I'll be there in forty-two minutes." Brax hung-up and threw on clothes. He grabbed his go-bag from his closet, which was actually a precisely filled backpack, and hauled ass to his Jeep. God willing, and the creek don't rise, he'd be at base in thirty-seven minutes, forty-two minutes since he got the call.

Of course, Kostya was already in the ready room.

He was always there first. Gideon still wasn't, which was unusual. Brax had beat half of his team members. Braxton spotted the coffee, and he knew Kostya had started it. Lord, love the man. Brax went to the table and poured himself a cup.

Ryker McQueen sidled up next to him. "The one good thing? Our backpacks are lighter, since we're headed to a warm climate."

"Yeah, but monsoon season is close to starting." Brax frowned. "Normally starts in May, but it decided to come a little earlier this year."

"Yeah, I've got my rain gear," Ryker said as he grabbed his mug of coffee.

Brax knew his team. Everybody had their rain gear; there wasn't a single man who wouldn't have checked the weather on where they were going. Of course, Kostya, being Kostya, would have rain gear next to the weapons, just in case.

Brax looked around for Nolan O'Roarke and spotted him just as he was entering the room. His pack was bigger than the rest of theirs. He and Gideon always had to pack more. Gideon, as the communications guy, had more equipment, and Nolan, as the medic, had bulked up with medical supplies and anything he could think of for any injury that might come his way.

Brax would bet the last dollar in his savings account Nolan had one or two changes of clothes for Jenny Rivers in his pack that he'd gotten from his wife, Maggie. Maggie wouldn't have asked a single question; she would've just offered things up. Plus, Nolan would have a set of rain gear and boots for the woman. That was just his friends' way.

Walking over to him, he caught Nolan's eye and held out his hand. "Give me."

"What are you talking about?"

"You've already got enough shit in your pack with all the medical gear. Give me all the clothes and shit you've got for Jenny Rivers. I'll carry that."

Nolan frowned at him. "This is my purview."

"I agree, you carrying the extra fifteen pounds of medical shit is part of your job. Carrying an extra eleven to sixteen pounds for Ms. Rivers? Don't think so. It's just stupid. Now give me."

Nolan rolled his eyes and put his pack on one of the desks, and Braxton put his beside it. Nolan took out all the gear he had for Jenny and Brax transferred it into his pack. As he shifted he realized that with the boots it was probably closer to fifteen pounds.

He grinned. "At least this way you won't have Kostya telling you to do this in front of everybody in twenty minutes."

"There is that," Nolan agreed.

Brax sat down next to Lincoln Hart and continued to eye both the door and Kostya. Gideon had now shown up so his lieutenant kept looking at whatever Gideon was showing him on his tablet. Kostya was not happy,

"Brax, shut off the lights, will you?" Kostya asked.

"But everybody's not here."

"Yes, they are." Kostya said.

So, we're going in lean. Good to know.

"Five bodies were discovered three days ago. Caucasian and African American. They were identified as the five men who work for Lowry Kidnap and Rescue, an outfit out of Texas. They're good."

Brax saw a couple of his teammates nod, as they all looked around to see who was missing, and who would actually be going on the mission.

"This is who Ms. Rivers' company, New Era Cyber Tech, hired to find her and bring her back. Their bodies got tangled in a fishing net. They'd been weighted down, but their bodies bloating brought them close to the surface. That's why they were found so quickly."

Gideon stayed on the shot of the bodies for just a moment before switching to a picture of two Bangladeshi women. "These are the two women who were with Ms. Rivers before she disappeared. Their story so far has been that they dropped off their brother and Ms. Rivers at her house then drove to their parents' home in Dhaka. That has never held water, and now with the five Lowry men showing up murdered, the US Embassy in Bangladesh brought the women in for further questioning."

Kostya looked around the room and when he was satisfied that everyone was tracking, he continued.

"Once the sisters were separated, we got the information we needed. We found out why they had never come forward. One of the women told the embassy personnel that Ms. Rivers had been taken by two men in police uniforms."

Gideon turned his chair away from his computer so he was looking at the team. "That would be the reason they weren't saying anything. If they saw their brother being murdered by the police, who can sometimes be the goon squads of the Awami League, they knew they would be in trouble. When the other sister was confronted with her sister's confession, they both started talking."

"Do you have their statements?" Jase asked.

"Yeah," Gideon said. "I've been going over them since eight last night. They said Ms. Rivers was taken away in a small delivery truck. She said it had writing and a logo on it, but it was too far away from them to make out the words. One of the sisters thinks the logo had a bull on it, but she wasn't positive."

"And?" Linc asked.

Everyone on the team knew Gideon hadn't left it at that. It wasn't in his nature.

"In the national firms, it was mostly banking and securities that use a bull in their logo, but they don't use delivery trucks like the women described. Currently, I'm scrolling through the online Bangladesh Yellow Pages to see if there are any businesses with a bull in their logo."

"They have yellow pages? Like those big books they used to deliver to our house and Mom used for the littler kids to sit on at the dinner table?" Jase asked.

"We don't have time for the snark, Jase," Kostya said. "Gideon, continue."

"The online Yellow Pages are where most local businesses in and around Dhaka advertise their business. They use text and artwork. I set up a program to identify logos with bulls in them. Hopefully, we'll have a match soon."

"In the meantime," Kostya said, "We go in. We would have liked to go with the backing of the Bangladeshi government, but that's not possible."

"Why?" Brax asked.

"Confessing that we basically had sanctioned mercenaries in their country would cause a shitload of trouble for our diplomats. They want this buried."

"Then why say they're ours? Couldn't they be victims of the civil unrest?" Brax pushed.

"One of the dumbasses got caught with their passports. Not only did it pin him as an American, it also showed that he'd just come into the country."

All of the men in the room grumbled.

"I thought they were better than that," Jase finally piped up.

"Apparently not." Kostya grimaced.

"How are we going in?" Brax asked.

Gideon switched to a new slide. It was an aerial shot of a lake and surrounding forest.

"HALO jump into the forested area surrounding Kaptai Lake, since that's where the mercenaries' bodies were found. We're going in here. It's the furthest point away from the resort and the temple." Kostya pointed to both things. "It's monsoon season, but according to the weather forecast, there is supposed to be a letup on the rain for twelve hours."

Each member of the small team was taking notes.

"Based on the murder of the Americans, and that Ms. Rivers' company sent in a Kidnap and Rescue company, we no longer think that this has anything to do with the unrest in the region. We think this is a simple kidnapping," Kostya said.

"Has anybody been able to confirm that?" Ryker McQueen wanted to know.

Kostya shook his head. "This morning, authorities will visit with the CEO of New Era Cyber Tech in DC to confirm this is a kidnapping. Then we'll know a lot more. We'll be briefed in the air."

"Are we just guessing this is where Ms. Rivers is being kept, based on where the Kidnap and Rescue team was found?" There was Brax's friend, Mateo Arundo, the consummate optimist.

"That about sums it up," their lieutenant confirmed.

"This should be fun," Jase grinned. "Are we leaving now?"

"As soon as the plane is ready."

Brax's lips twitched as his gaze roamed the room. Jase pulled out his iPhone and two big brick power back-ups to make sure his iPhone had plenty of back-up power. It used to be he'd play video games and movies during the entire long flights, but Brax would bet his bottom dollar some of those movies were now of Bonnie and Jase's kids. His teammate was now a total family man. Brax thought back to Jase and Bonnie's wedding, where Jase's sixteen brothers and sisters had shown up. It had been a blast.

Brax didn't even need to look at Linc and Nolan. He knew if both the men had their Kindles, they'd be set. Men after his own heart. Gideon would be poring over his tablet, taking in as much new information as possible, and then discussing probabilities and new avenues of attack with Kostya.

Ryker would either be asleep or talking. That was him. He was always either on or off. As for Mateo, he took out his iPhone and looked at his screensaver. Of course, it was of Lainey. It was a damn good picture. Brax had known Mateo pre-Lainey; the difference was night and day. It'd be interesting to see how he spent his time during this flight.

Brax had his pen and notebook. It would mean nothing if it got into enemy hands. Just some of the same old scribblings he'd done for years. When he got home, he'd toss the full notebook in the pile with the rest. Then read a *real* science fiction book and realize he really couldn't write worth shit, but at least it kept his mind occupied.

5

ANOTHER WRACKING COUGH WOKE HER UP. JENNY wondered how long she'd slept this time. Ten minutes or ten hours. Did it matter? All she could hear was the ever-present rain pelting the tin roof of the shack.

She shifted, then groaned in pain. But she needed to get away from the leak in the shack's roof. But where wasn't there a leak? Her hand splatted in the mud. She lifted it up to the stream of water to rinse it. When it was clean, she could push back her hair from her face and do her best to tie her hair into a braid again, so it wasn't straggled all over.

She must have slept for a few hours because her motor skills were better than the last time she'd tried to braid her hair. Her coughing made long work of her project. She'd been coughing forever. The best she could figure is that it had been going on for at least seven days, and it had become more bronchial in the last three. She was trying to spit up as much mucus as possible, but she felt more and more of it just settling and rattling in her chest.

Her laugh was hoarse and harsh as she thought of the next time they took a picture for their proof of life. How were they going to make her corpse look lively next to the Dhaka Tribune? She laughed harder as she thought of the pointy-faced prick who always picked her up by her hair realizing she was dead. Yeah, he'd sure be up shit creek with that fat son-of-a-bitch in charge then.

She started coughing again. It was so bad that she felt like her ribs might crack. She leaned over and ended up right where she started, rain pouring down the back of her neck. She tried to focus between the tumultuous hacking of her body and the searing pain in her ribs. Then she remembered a song by one of her idols.

Something about preferring to be dry, but at least she was alive.

As soon as she could breathe, Jenny starting singing.

"Rain on me. Rain on me."

"Wake up!"

"Wake up!"

Someone was twisting the hair off her head.

"I said, wake up!"

Jenny opened her eyes and looked up at a man who

looked scared. He turned away from her. "I told you she was alive."

He was still holding her braid in his fist.

"Hurry and take the picture," he yelled.

The flash of light shot through her eyes, into her brain, and Jenny screamed. If the tiny moan she heard could be considered a scream. She hurt. She hurt so bad.

"She's going to die, and we're not going to be paid. I should kill you now."

"She's fine."

She was pulled up higher; now she was on her knees. "See, she's almost standing."

Through her haze Jenny could make out some of the Bangla language, not much, but enough. Thank God she'd taken her job seriously and did her best to learn the language. But dammit, not enough!

Shut up! At least they want me alive!

Jenny started coughing, and all hope of understanding what they were saying was whisked away as she did her best to hold in the worst of it so that she wouldn't literally break a rib. But she was sure she already had.

When she could breathe again, she felt two men on either side of her. They both reached under one of her armpits and lifted her up.

Jenny cried out in agonizing pain as fire ripped up her left side.

Ribs punctured lungs, right?
How?

They were dragging her out of the shack and for the first time in what felt like years she was outside. It was monsoon season and there was mud and rain, but she was outside. She moaned with pleasure. The cold water felt so good on her fevered skin, she never wanted to go indoors again. Then she started to shiver. As soon as she had that thought, she was thrust through the door of what looked like some kind of mobile home or trailer.

Jenny landed face first on damp carpet.

"Hey!"

"What are you doing?"

They were two unfamiliar voices.

"You're the brains of this outfit. You think you know everything about how to get us money? Well, Rakib wants you to keep her alive so that we get our money. Good luck with that."

Jenny heard the door shut behind her, then there was dead quiet, until she started to cough.

"What's wrong with her?" the voice asked. He sounded young.

"How should I know?" somebody else answered.

"We need her alive." The young voice spoke again.

"I know that!" Despite the yelling, the older man was gently rolling Jenny over. "Can you talk?" he asked her in English.

She groaned as he rolled her onto her injured rib, the groan turned into great hacking coughs.

She heard him shout, "When was the last time she drank? Get her some water."

Jenny cringed at the idea of more water when she was finally in a place where she wasn't being rained on.

"Miss, lift up your head. You need to drink."

Huh? What's he talking about?

Sandpaper hands pushed her forehead backward, and a bottle pressed against her lips. As the first drop of the untainted water hit her tongue she reached up to grab the bottle, but her arms were too weak.

"Easy, Miss. Let us help you."

Her two functioning brain cells told her they just wanted to help her so they could get their ransom, but she didn't care. She was dying of thirst, even as dirty rainwater poured into the hut. Ingesting clean water was survival. That's all her life had come down to since she had been dumped in the back of that meat truck.

Survival.

"She's shivering. Get a blanket."

"It's not going to be of any use, with all those wet clothes."

"I'm not going to undress her, are you?" the older man asked.

Jenny sent up a silent prayer of thanks. She didn't know the name of the one guard who was constantly pushing and pulling at her. The guard who, so far, had never been alone with her. But that pig definitely wanted to undress her.

If he rapes me, I think I'll just drown myself in the mud.

"Turn on the floor heater, and let's put her near it," the older man said. He was trying to gently move her away from the door, where she had originally been thrown, but it didn't matter how gentle he tried to be. It hurt. Everything. Everywhere. Her whole body *hurt*.

Jenny shifted her toes in her right boot and cried

out in pain. When was the last time she'd taken her boots and socks off and lifted her feet up to the running water coming from the ceiling to wash them? How many mini showers had she attempted to give her different body parts in futile hopes of staying healthy?

Now that she was out of her shack, had some clean water to drink, and a dry spot, she couldn't think of anything good. She hurt too much. Jenny finally realized just how bad her coughing and fever chills were. Maybe she wouldn't survive after all.

"She looks better."

It was the leader. She'd seen him a couple of times. He was a fat man. Everybody bowed and scraped around him.

"Get the hair out of her face so I can see her eyes, then take the picture."

Before anyone could touch her, Jenny pushed her hair back behind her ears, grateful that it was now finally dry.

"Hold this." Somebody shoved a newspaper into her hands. She looked at the date.

It wasn't possible. There was no way that only three weeks had gone by. It felt like she had been taken a year ago.

As she held up the paper in front of her, drops of blood marred the Dhaka Tribune.

The flash of a camera went off and she winced.

"What is wrong with her?" The leader demanded an answer.

"Her nose is bleeding," a young man said. She recognized him. He'd given her a blanket and water and food. Soft food, because her mouth hurt.

"Why is her nose bleeding?"

"Who knows," somebody answered. "We're going to get our payment any day. Then we won't need her anymore."

Jenny knew her expression didn't change. She'd stopped letting them get to her after the first forty-eight hours of captivity. It was like with her dad, she never wanted them to know what she was thinking or feeling. And, anyway, they'd been talking about not needing her for a long time now. Hadn't they figured out her company wasn't going to pay up?

"Are you sure they'll finally pay?" the old man asked.

Shit. He shouldn't have asked the leader that. That was a sure way to get yourself killed. She'd seen it happen.

"After their men disappeared? I'm sure," Rakib, the leader, finally answered. "Now that she's had all this nice time in the trailer, put her back in the shack."

Jenny's heart plummeted. She might have told herself she could handle anything, but the idea of being in that six-inch-deep mud, with the bucket for a toilet and wet naan for a meal almost did have her in tears.

She looked down when she felt more drips, afraid she was crying in front of the leader. But they weren't tear drops, they were more drops of blood from her nose. This couldn't be good.

Gideon had gotten them more intel by the time they dropped in. They no longer were just aiming for the same area where the K&R bodies were found. Finally, New Era Cyber Tech was talking to the Department of Homeland Security. They confessed that Jenny Rivers had indeed been kidnapped, and that there was a ransom request. Bangladesh was a shitshow right now. Too many competing factions trying to take over the country, and that made it damn near impossible to determine who to talk to about Jenny's kidnapping.

The US Embassy had already sent home all non-essential employees, so Omega Sky was depending on the locals and remaining embassy personnel who had been in place for years for intel. These were the people who would have knowledge of who had kidnapped Jenny Rivers, and where they might be headquartered.

As soon as all of the team had landed, and each one of them had been sure to stash or hide their parachute in a spot where it wouldn't be found, they met up.

"Where to?" Jase asked casually. He sounded like he was about to take a day's hike in the woods and then go roast hotdogs and have s'mores later.

Gideon took his precious tablet out from his pack. "Mark this, in case we get separated." He provided the coordinates. "We received some intelligence that there is a band of Bangladeshi mercenaries operating five clicks east of Silchari. That gives them some road access, but then they have enough forest coverage to be invisible."

Gideon blew up a satellite image of the small village of Silchari. They could see the areas that must be crops, a few homes, and a narrow road. Having some kind of mercenary headquarters nearby made sense.

Brax looked up and saw ominous rain clouds to the east. Right now the rain was mild. Soon it would be torrential.

Jase took point and Kostya took up the rear, with Gideon right in front of him. They would stop every three hours to see if Gideon got any updates, using his equipment connected to satellites. His tablet was bulletproof. Well, maybe not bulletproof, but it could take a licking and keep on ticking. The monsoon didn't stop it.

"Anything new?" Kostya asked on their fifth stop when Gideon was avidly studying his tablet.

"I've got a photo, two days old, that the kidnappers sent to her company for proof of life. The company has transferred a third of the ransom in cryptocurrency to their account. That was today. My guess is that is just going to piss off the mercenaries, and they're going to do something to show they mean business to get the rest of the money."

Brax looked around and saw how everybody was taking the information. All of them were looking over Gideon's shoulder to see the picture of Jenny holding up the newspaper with the date on it. It was two days ago. She looked awful. It was clear she was extremely sick. Even if they got there by 0400, would she still be alive? And what was with her company? Why were they dicking around with the ransom? They knew that five men had died trying to rescue her.

"Boss, she's not going to make it," Nolan said what the rest of them were thinking. "By the looks of it she's either been beaten badly and we just can't see it, or she's suffering from an infection. By the flush on her face, and the glassy eyes and the nosebleed, my bet is infection."

Brax looked closer at the picture and he saw exactly what Nolan was talking about.

"Do you have antibiotics that can help her?" Brax asked.

He nodded. "But we'll need to get her to a hospital, fast."

Everybody nodded. Brax took one last look at her picture and sent up a prayer. She reminded him of CiCi and how desperately ill she had been so many times. Fuck picking up the pace, he wanted to start running.

Mateo nudged him. "You okay?"

It was funny how much he'd bonded with the guy after the near miss at Gideon's place eight months ago. Before, he'd have said Nolan was his go-to guy, but now it was a toss-up.

"Just worried about Jenny."

"You were looking at her pretty intensely. Bringing up thoughts of your sister?"

Okay, maybe he was closer to Mateo than he realized.

"Yeah. I can't stand that she's sick, and that she's been abandoned like she has."

"Abandoned?"

"By her fucking company. What are they thinking, only paying a third of the ransom? Are they stupid?"

"Homeland Security will straighten them out," Mateo assured him.

"Yeah, but soon enough?"

They looked at one another. They both knew that the kidnappers were likely to escalate to get the rest of their money.

"Listen up," Kostya raised his voice so everybody could hear him. "Change of plans. Now that we have the intel that we need, we're going to do this double time. I want us to get there by dawn. I don't care if we have to hit them during daylight. We'll do what we have to get our target out of there safe, sound, and whole."

Brax grinned, and when he looked around, he saw everybody else grinning as well.

6

Jenny shut her eyes and imagined herself enjoying making mud pies. She knew she had enjoyed doing it when she had grown up in Wyoming. At least for a little while. Before getting dirty was a bad thing. Before everything she did was a bad thing.

She scooped up a glop of mud and tried to form it into a mud pie, but it was no use. It was too runny. So much for recreating a childhood memory.

She started singing the rain song.

"Rain on me. Rain on me."

She pretended it was only rain streaking down her face and not tears. Then the coughing started up again, and she moaned at the pain in her chest, and the stabbing pain from her rib.

She swiped at her face and saw blood on her hand.

My nose.

Too bad she didn't have WebMD to figure out why her damn nose was bleeding. Then she could hypochondriac herself to death.

She laughed. Which set off an even worse bout of coughing. Jenny tried to remain upright. She didn't want to lie down in the mud. It got in her hair, and sometimes her ears and mouth. She felt herself slipping sideways along the wall. She covered her ear and closed her eyes, hoping she wouldn't drown in mud.

"THREE VEHICLES. A box truck with a logo of a bull on it, an SUV, and a van. Lots of men and weapons," Brax could barely hear Jase say through his comm device. The monsoon was out of control, and the rain was making things almost impossible, including their ability to communicate.

"Give me a number," Kostya demanded.

"I see nine. But there's a barracks, three shacks and it looks like they've hauled in a trailer, which should be their command center. It has a satellite. My guess is this isn't their first rodeo."

"So, there is a road that wasn't on the satellite images," Brax growled loudly into his mic. Even with his poncho, the rain was pummeling his face as it came down sideways.

"Must have been small and covered by the trees, I didn't see it," Gideon said.

"If there is a trailer, barracks, and encampment, how did the satellite photos not pick it up?" Brax wanted to know.

"Most of it is under camouflage netting. They have

a satellite dish on top of the trailer. That's how they are accessing the internet." Jase answered.

"That's all I can see. Linc, you need to tell us the rest," Jase said to their sniper who was now in a tall tree.

"I'm counting eleven. The barracks looks like it houses sixteen by my estimate. The trailer would be the command center, but it would also be where the leader stays."

"The shacks?" Kostya asked.

"Only one has a padlock on it," Linc answered.

"Then we have our target."

Everybody heard the satisfaction in Kostya's voice. Brax could almost hear him thinking. They all knew what needed to happen. They needed to get her piece off the chessboard first, so that she was protected, then they could go in and clean up.

"If I could be one of the ones to help get her out, then I could set that shack to blow as well as the others," Brax said.

Kostya gave him a considering look, then slowly smiled. "I like it."

"I need to be there to help get her out. We won't know what shape she's in," Nolan chimed in.

Brax nodded. "Good call."

God, let her be alive. I'm begging you. Let her be alive.

"Linc, stay in position where you can protect both of them if needed."

"Got it."

"The rest of us, we'll surround their bunker. As soon as we hear from Nolan that he has Ms. Rivers out of there, and Brax has everything set to blow, I'll give the order to start our assault. Linc, you focus on everyone who comes out of the barracks."

"I can do that," Brax said.

"Negative." Kostya shook his head. "By the looks of her on that last proof of life, Ms. Rivers is going to require immediate help. I want her in Chattogram as soon as possible, and as far away from this assault as possible. Your job is to acquire a vehicle and work with Nolan to get her the fuck out of there."

Made sense.

Brax nodded. He looked over at his friend through the rain, who gave him a worried smile. Brax's heart sank. It wasn't often that Nolan was worried about a patient. He always thought he could win the war and keep someone alive until they got to a hospital. His hesitation was not good. Not good at all.

Brax sidled up to him. "What's got you so worried?" he asked out of the side of his mouth.

"Infection and pneumonia. That nosebleed says she's probably coughing hard enough to break some blood vessels in her nose, ones that are already fragile from infection and severe dehydration. We're close to the end if we don't get to her soon."

"Don't say that," was Brax's vehement response. "You always have some voodoo. I've seen you put men's guts back into their stomach and keep them alive. You have this."

Nolan stood up straighter. "You're right. I have this."

"Okay, men. Let's move."

Brax gave a sigh of relief at Kostya's command. He needed to get to Jenny.

Now.

JENNY'S RACKING cough woke her up. She started to cry as she attempted to wipe her eyes, and smeared more mud into them instead. She looked up and found another hole in the shack where rain was pouring through. She closed her eyes, moved under it, and let it wash her face. She was dying of thirst but was too afraid to drink the rainwater. God knew what it picked up from the roof.

At least I'm going to die with a clean face.

She hiccupped as another sob wrenched through her body. Somehow, she had enough strength to push herself up so she could lean against the wall of the shack. Sitting was too much to ask for.

I'm going to die, and I did a piss-poor job of living.

Tina. Tina always tried to stay in touch after college, but Jenny never had time for her old roommate. She was too busy trying to climb the corporate ladder. Even Jarrod, her brief boyfriend who had turned into a good friend, tried his best to hold on to their friendship, but Jenny had blown him off, too, until they fell out of touch. As far as current friends, Jenny could count them on one hand. Tina from college. Fiona from work when she was in London for Cyber Tech, up until Fiona left. Sabina was a brand new work friend, she supposed. And who else?

One hand? More like I can almost count my friends on one finger.

She'd been sad when her mom had died, but it had been like she'd died years before her actual death. Her dad? He couldn't have died soon enough, as far as Jenny was concerned.

Work friends. I had a career and a handful of work friends wherever I went. What a waste of a life.

"Come on, you saw the world. You had adventures."

Jenny bit her lip and dropped her head.

Such a waste.

She looked down at the mud and huffed out a laugh. This was her destiny. Death by mud.

"Fuck that shit! Quit with the maudlin and pull up your bootstraps!"

She looked around the shack.

"Who said that?"

She laughed. She'd said that. The problem was she couldn't recognize the voice because she sounded like she'd been smoking five packs a day since she was a ten-year-old.

I'm right. I do need to quit with the boo-hoo.

She did her best to shove upward so she was sitting up. "I'm not going to die in mud. NECT has Kidnapping and Rescue, and if that doesn't work, they'll pay up."

"Keep it down in there. You need to be quiet."

"Who said that?"

Great, now I'm hallucinating. Figures.

She took a deep breath, trying to get her head on straight, then started hacking up a lung. She clutched her torso, trying to keep from jostling her rib, but it was no use. Spikes of agony sparked along every nerve ending until she was crying out in pain between coughs.

"Honey, can you try to be quiet? Just for a little bit."

"Who are you?"

She heard the padlock being jostled. *Great, time for another picture.* They'd have to carry her out of here this time. There was no way she could walk.

Then she heard something at the back of the shack. It sounded like something was cutting and pulling at some boards that made up the back wall. She watched as three small boards were cut out, a little larger than a cupboard.

Weird.

"Ms. Rivers, it's time to go."

She looked at the glittering eyes that were mostly covered by a rubber or plastic poncho. She heard what he said, but he made no sense.

"Go where?"

"Ms. Rivers, we don't have much time. Come over here and crawl out, and we'll take you to safety."

The mercenaries didn't wear ponchos like that. "Who are you?"

"I'm Braxton Walker, I'm a member of the United States Navy. I'm here with my team, and our job is to get you out of here. Now please get over here so we can finish our mission."

This has to be a hallucination. I'm drowning to death in the mud.

"Jenny, did you hear me?"

"You're not real."

"I am real, and I need you to get over here."

Maybe he was real. She could hear the urgency in his voice.

"I'm sorry, but if you are real, this won't work. I can barely sit up, let alone crawl over there. This won't work."

He looked at her for what seemed like an eternity. Finally, he said, "I understand." He backed out of the hole and she was just left looking at the pouring rain.

Jenny stared at the hole. That man had to be real, didn't he? There was a hole in the wall, so that meant he was real, right? He didn't just disappear, did he?

She heard the same sawing and pulling and soon the hole was bigger. The man. What was his name? Oh yeah. Braxton. He was crawling into her muddy shack. He was fast. "Okay Jenny, let's get you out of here." He crouched down beside her, then put one arm beneath her legs and one arm around her back and picked her up like she weighed nothing. Her head lolled down, like her neck was broken.

"Shit." He shifted, then somehow her head was resting against his chest. It felt good to be resting on the clean water of his poncho. He strode over to the hole and crouched down again. Then he threaded her through the passage and another set of arms gently picked her up into the same kind of hold. This man also held her so that her head was resting against his chest.

Who were these men?

Vaguely, she noticed the first man was standing up next to her. "I'm going to set the charges. Start heading to the side of the camp with the vehicles. As soon as I'm done, I'm going for a vehicle. Hopefully, you'll be there by the time I've procured one."

"Got it," the man holding her said.

The first man left like he had never been there. The man carrying her looked down into her face. "Ms. Rivers, I'm going to have to set a fast pace to get us out of the line of fire and into a good position to take off in one of the vehicles. It's going to be a rough ride, can you handle it?"

"Yes." Her voice was so hoarse, she wondered if he could hear her.

"Is there any way you could ride piggyback along my front? We could make better time."

Jenny felt the tears coming as she shook her head. She was useless.

"It's not a problem. We can get this done. You know the SEAL motto. The only easy day was yesterday. We've got this."

Well, that answered that question. They were SEALs. Maybe there was hope, after all.

7

THE PLAN HAD BEEN THAT WHEN THE MERCENARY CAMP was taken care of, Allen could land the helicopter and extract them. But in this sideways torrential downpour? Kostya wouldn't risk it when there were other means to get them out of there, like the vehicles.

When Braxton got the third charge set, he drifted back into the forest, careful that nobody saw him. As soon as he lost sight of the clearing, he ran around to the west side so that he could commandeer a ride. Out of everybody, he was the fastest at hot-wiring a car. He'd even beat out the geek, Gideon.

It had to do with how good he was with munitions. Brax could hot-wire anything with wheels. But maybe he wouldn't have to if this crew left the keys in one of the normal spots. On top of the wheels, under the sun visor and, of course, the glove box. He got to the vehicles and headed to the first one, a Toyota Land Cruiser. That would work best, and he'd leave the van for the rest of the men. Since they drove on the left side of the road, the cars had the steering wheels on the wrong side as far as Brax was concerned, but it worked to his advantage this time. The passenger's side was parallel to the clearing, so he looked on top of the passenger side tires. No keys. He tried the driver's door, and it was open. As soon as he did, he softly laughed.

There was always option four, leave the keys in the ignition.

"Nolan," he said into his mic. "I've got our vehicle. It's a Land Cruiser. We can push down the two back seats and you'll have enough room to maneuver with her. Give me your position and I'll come help carry her."

"I'm almost to your position. Wait there," Nolan responded.

"Is everybody in place?" Kostya asked. Everyone muttered yes. "Brax, how much longer before the charges go?"

Brax looked down at his watch and waited ten seconds to answer. "Four minutes exactly."

"I'm here," Nolan said through the driver's side window. "I'll go through the back."

"Hold on, I'll push back the rear seats so you can work on her when she's flat."

Nolan nodded.

Brax maneuvered to the back and pushed the seats down. The entire vehicle was filthy, but it was a hell of a lot better than the slurry of mud that was in the shack she'd been kept in. When he spied a tarp he grinned. Even better. He pushed the debris to the end of the

Land Cruiser and placed the tarp out so Nolan could work on Jenny.

"Speed it up." Nolan slammed his fist against the tailgate. Brax opened it and carefully took Jenny from Nolan's arms and placed her down on the tarp. He yanked off his backpack and fished out his change of shirt, skivvies, and socks. He wrapped the underwear and socks into his shirt, and created a semblance of a pillow for her. Nolan gave him the side-eye as he pushed him out of the way.

She started to cough. Deep bronchial coughs that had her moaning in pain as she clutched her right side. Where her ribs were.

"Punctured lung?" Brax asked Nolan.

"No, she wouldn't be able to cough like she is. Right now—"

Explosions rocked the land cruiser, and Jenny groaned in pain again. It was heart-wrenching.

"Drive!" Kostya yelled through the comm.

The sound of rapid assault rifles going off was deafening. Brax scrambled between the passenger and driver's seat, got situated, then started the engine.

He'd already scoped out where the road was, and of course the truck was pointing away from it. There was no way he was going to circle around or even do a three-point turn; he didn't want to do anything that might put them in the line of fire. Fuck, he was going to have to get the hell out of here driving in reverse. He wouldn't have done this; except he'd seen he had a rear windshield wiper.

As soon as he slammed the SUV into reverse, the

rearview camera went into action and it displayed everything behind him. That's not how he drove. He threw his left hand over the seat, and looked backward, and hit the accelerator. It didn't move.

Fuck!

Too much mud, dumbass. Start slower.

Brax went slowly forward two meters, then started backward again, not in the same grooves as before or as fast. He grinned as he made headway. He looked around and saw that no one was looking his way.

Perfect.

He picked up speed.

Crack!

A bullet went through one of the back windows.

"You okay?" he yelled.

"We're fine. Keep driving," Nolan yelled back. Despite his words, Brax heard the stress in his friend's voice. Things were bad back there. Well, hell, they were pretty fucking bad up here. Brax couldn't see shit with the rain pummeling down, even with the windshield wiper. He looked down at the rearview display and concentrated on that. It was better.

Brax grit his teeth as he attempted to stay on what could loosely be described as a road. He jerked at the wheel when he got too close to a tree.

Fuck!

The truck slid in the mud, and Brax did the same maneuvers as if he were driving in snow. He went with the slide, and gently steered the vehicle away from the trees on the other side of the trail. He could feel the sweat running down the back of his neck. He got the

SUV straightened and kept going. He looked around him. He couldn't see the clearing.

"Linc!" he shouted. "Are we clear?"

"Yeah. You can stop and wait for the rest of us. We're almost done cleaning house," he replied.

"No!" Nolan spat. "Jenny needs to get to a hospital. Now! Brax, keep driving. Can you get this thing turned around?"

"Not now, maybe we'll get to a wider spot where I can." He sent up a prayer to the God who had saved CiCi.

"Then keep going," Nolan ordered.

So he did.

JENNY TRIED to open her eyes, but it hurt. Everything hurt. Something was wrapped tightly around her upper arm. She felt someone touching the inside of her elbow, rubbing it. She smelled alcohol. Then she felt a sharp sting like something horrible has stung her, followed by pressure. Whatever was wrapped around her upper arm loosened. Then whoever it was who hurt her arm touched her chest and she flinched.

Not now. Please don't do this to me now.

She tried to push the hands away, but her arms felt like over-cooked pasta and she knew she couldn't do anything to protect herself.

"Stop. No." She whimpered the two words. She had to fight, even if it was only with words.

"Ms. Rivers, I need to examine you, then I need to

get you dried off and dress you in something dry and warm before we get some saline into you. Okay?"

Her shirt was being pulled up. What was left of it. She'd torn off some to stop the bleeding on the back of her head, and then her nose. When the man—and it was a man, she'd heard him—pulled her shirt over her head, she shot up a knee.

There. I can fight back. Hopefully I hurt the bastard.

Then she felt cold metal at her chest and she whimpered again.

"Please. No. Don't kill me."

There was a tug, then her breasts fell out of her bra for the first time in weeks.

"Ahhh!" Pain sliced through her torso. Had he slid his knife through her side?

"I'm sorry, Ms. Rivers, I know your ribs have to be killing you."

Why is this scum calling me Ms. Rivers?

"After I get you cleaned up, I'll bandage them up, then give you a shirt to wear, okay?"

He sounds nice.

Wait a minute. He sounds American!

"Who are you?" She croaked out the question.

"Chief Petty Officer Nolan O'Roarke, Omega Sky SEAL Team, United States Navy."

She huffed out a laugh, then started coughing. When she finally stopped, she opened her eyes. "You could have said Nolan."

She saw him grin down at her. "I guess I could have." He might be grinning but she could see his tension behind the grin. That couldn't be good. She looked at her arm and saw that what she thought had been something stinging her was an IV line. It was attached to long tubing that snaked up to a bag hanging from a coat hook above the vehicle's window.

"How bad is it?" she asked.

"Your ribs hurt, don't they?"

"Are you a doctor?"

"Medic."

"Then on a score of one to ten, when I cough the pain is at one-hundred. Does that help?"

Nolan sighed. "I'm not sure how many are broken, but that cough has done a number on your ribs."

As if to prove his point she started to cough so hard her entire body spasmed. Her throat filled with mucus and she looked up at the man who was leaning over her and swallowed it.

"Ms. Rivers, you've got to get rid of the phlegm, it's the best thing you can do for yourself." He held a bottle of water to her lips. As soon as she was done drinking, she thanked him.

She gave him the best smile she could under the circumstances. "Am I going to live?"

"Damn right you are!" the driver shouted. "We didn't run through the jungle to have you die on us now."

Jenny started to cough again. The man up front continued to yell at her. "You better spit that shit out. Get all of that phlegm out of your lungs. Pretend it's a spitting contest and the prize is a million bucks. This is no time to be ladylike."

In between coughs, Jenny laughed, then she rolled

over and found Nolan holding out a towel for her to spit into. She hated this. Fucking hated this, but now that she was spared drowning in mud, she sure as hell wasn't going to drown in her own spit!

She heard her chest rattle. She kept coughing and coughing and coughing. How much mucus could one body create?

"That's good, Ms. Rivers," Nolan said. "Are you allergic to cephalosporins?"

"No."

"Good." He took a fat syringe filled with fluid out of his bag. "I'm going to give you a cephalosporin push to get it onboard faster." He screwed the syringe into her IV and spent the next couple of minutes pushing the plunger down until it was empty, then he unscrewed it from the IV. After that, he tapped her back, then started to rub it. It was odd. It took a while for Jenny to realize he was using a wet cloth. Thank God, she might finally get clean.

When she finally stopped coughing, Nolan helped her sit up. Her arms were too weak to cover her breasts. And really, who cared at this point? He'd just seen her spit and snort out a gallon of snot and mucus, having him look at her breasts was three steps up.

"Ms. Rivers, do you want to wash up your front before putting on the clean shirt?"

Jenny looked down at her mud-covered torso. Tears of frustration welled as she realized she was too weak to even wash herself.

"I can't. My arms are too heavy."

"I can help. My wife insists on me giving our

toddler, Iris, baths at least three times a week when I'm home." He smiled. "Actually, I'm the one who insists. I love how Iris likes to play in the tub, of course clean-up is always a chore."

Jenny appreciated how he was attempting to make her feel comfortable. "If you could help me wash, I'd appreciate it," she whispered.

"We can get this done real fast, then get you into a clean shirt in no time, I promise.

Nolan was as good as his word. Before she could form a question about his daughter, he was done.

"Now I'll pretend you're my daughter and get you into this shirt. We can get this done, easy-peasy." He undid the tubing from the IV, put the shirt over her head, then easily threaded her arms through the sleeves. He took out an alcohol swab, cleaned the IV, and reattached the tubing. The smaller bag was half-empty now.

"There you go, you're all set. How do you feel?"

"Like I might live," she rasped out.

"Damn right you will," the driver yelled. "Hold on back there, I'm going to turn us around."

Jenny would have fallen over if it hadn't been for Nolan grabbing her. But the whirl of the car was too much for her. She got so dizzy that she felt herself fade.

"Nolan?"

"Right here."

"Sorry."

She passed out.

8

Brax's satellite phone rang. It was Gideon.

"Jenny's alive. She's passed out, but Nolan's pumping her full of fluid and antibiotics."

"Good. That's good. But we've got a problem. Jase has been hit. It's not looking too good. We need Nolan."

Brax calculated that it had been half a klick back from where he had turned the SUV around. Before that he'd driven in reverse for maybe three klicks. This time, he could drive forward.

"I can get him to you in thirty minutes in this rain."

"We'll meet you halfway. We're in the van. Then we'll follow you."

"I need someone else to drive this when I go back to work on Jenny."

"Understood. It'll be Ryker."

Brax blew out a breath of relief. Ryker would be his choice of driver.

"Good. I'll get there as fast as I can," Brax told his second in command.

He put the SUV in reverse and sent up a prayer for Jase. Nothing could happen to him. Nothing. Not now that his friend was married to Bonnie and had two kids.

Not now, God. Not now.

As soon as he saw the break in the road that gave him more space, he yelled back. "Brace!" Then he made the three-point turn and skidded forward. Hopefully, whoever was driving the van with Jase in it had found another spot to turn around that he had missed.

"I've got your position," Gideon said over Brax's phone. "You're seventeen hundred meters ahead of us. Start slowing down." Gideon always had a lock on all of them. Their second in command tracking the members of Omega Sky had saved their asses on multiple occasions.

He heard Gideon yell at Ryker to slow down as well.

Brax took it easy. Now that he had built up a good speed, he didn't want to have the SUV skid again by hitting the brakes too hard.

Were those headlights ahead, or was he dreaming?

"Twelve hundred meters, Brax. You keep coming, we're backing up. We saw a place for you to turn around about a klick back."

"Can he wait that long?" Nolan asked from the back.

Now that they were within range of one another, their comm system worked, and the men with Gideon heard his question.

"He'll have to. We've got a tourniquet on his thigh. It just missed his femoral artery. But he still lost a fuck-ton of blood. He's shocky." That was Linc talking.

Brax closed his eyes for a second. They didn't have plasma with them, but they could definitely do blood transfusions. "Everyone's with you, right?"

"Right," Gideon answered.

Brax blew out a breath as he continued to slow down. There. There were the headlights. They were still backing up. He caught up and stayed at their speed.

"How's she doing?" Brax asked Nolan.

"Not conscious. She needs to rest, but at the same time, I need her to clear her lungs."

"How?" Brax asked.

"In addition to the saline drip, she's got to drink water. Lots and lots of water. That'll thin the sputum and help clear her lungs. That plus the broad spectrum antibiotics should do it for her in the next six hours before we get to Chattogram. But her fever is at one-oh-three and her blood pressure's in the basement. I'm worried about sepsis.

"Jeez."

"How close are we to Jase?"

"You better start packing up your kit, but leave behind what I need for Jenny. I'm going to be taking care of her when Ryker comes up here to drive."

"Gotcha."

One-oh-three. That was not good. When he'd picked her up in the shack, he could barely feel her. She felt lighter than his backpack.

"Stop," Kostya said through the comm link. "Nolan, get over here now."

Nolan already had his poncho on, and he was

jumping out the tailgate before the vehicle stopped. As fast as Nolan was running toward the other vehicle, Ryker was running to Brax's. Brax gave himself a shake and got the hell out of the driver's seat then shuffled his ass back to Jenny, making sure the tailgate was securely shut.

"You good back there?" Ryker yelled as he dropped into the driver's seat.

"We're good. Get this turned around and us out of here."

"Yes, boss."

Brax rolled his eyes. That was Ryker, always irreverent no matter the situation. Brax held onto Jenny so that she didn't slide around. As soon as Ryker had the SUV turned around, he yelled, "Incoming."

Brax looked up in time to catch his pack with one hand.

"What the fuck?"

"It's got most of our water. Figured she needed as much as you could get her to drink before we got to Chattogram."

Brax grinned as he looked down at the woman who was tucked in close to him. Ryker was right, he needed to wake her up.

"Jenny, I need you to wake up."

The leaves were beautiful. She loved fall in Appalachia. Especially when she could carve out a day to go hiking. Just her and nature. The hickory and maple trees were her favorite. Not just the color of their leaves, but their smell.

She took a deep breath. But she couldn't. It was like her head was covered by a plastic bag. She opened her eyes and saw a man looming over her.

"Get it off," she begged.

She tried to tear it off herself, but her arms wouldn't work.

She gasped for breath, but it didn't work. She couldn't breathe. Then she started to cough. Deep painful coughing that started in the middle of her body and spread throughout her limbs to her fingers and toes.

"That's it baby, cough out the nasty."

She felt herself being gently rolled to her stomach. Someone was carefully keeping her from touching the ground.

"Spit it all out, Jenny."

She kept coughing and coughing, and soon her body began to rattle, and she coughed up phlegm, and spit it into the towel that was below her face. All the time she'd been coughing, she felt a warm hand stroking her back. She was shivering so hard that the heat felt good.

"You done?" The voice asked.

Jenny nodded.

He rolled her back so that she was in his arms as he knelt. She looked around. She wasn't in a forest. Nope, it was the car. She was out of the shack. Looking up, she remembered this man. He was the one who had carried her out of the shack and then passed her onto another man.

"Who are you again?"

"Brax." He smiled.

"Where are we?"

"We're close to a village called Silchari. Hopefully we can stop there and get gas, a couple of blankets and maybe some more medical supplies before heading to the hospital in Chattogram."

She frowned, trying to remember a town called Silchari. It didn't ring any bells. Chattogram was one of the major cities in Bangladesh, so that city she'd heard of.

"Here, drink this." Brax rested the top of a bottle of water against her lips.

"I'm not thirsty."

"Doesn't matter. You have a fever and you're dehydrated. Now drink."

She tried, but could only stomach four small sips. "That's all I can handle. Any more and I'll throw up."

She almost could smile as she watched him grimace.

"What? You can handle all my gross spitting but not my puking?"

"Your spit doesn't stink."

This time she did smile. "Good point."

All the time she'd been in his arms, the SUV they were riding in had swerved and bumped. In one small way it reminded her of that first hellish ride in the butcher truck. But just in a small way. Being held by Brax made everything much better.

"You said I had a fever. What's wrong with me? Do you know?"

"Our medic thinks it's because you have pneumonia."

"Could it be because of another type of infection?"

He frowned down at her. "What other kind of infection?"

"When they first captured me, they threw me into the back of a butcher truck. There was animal blood all over the floor. I was tied up and thrown in, face down. It got all over my face and in my mouth and I inhaled some. I was pretty out of it to begin with."

Brax hit the mic on his comm unit. "Nolan, we've got a problem."

"Nolan can't answer now, he's working on Jase. What's your problem?" Kostya asked.

"Jenny thinks she inhaled animal blood on the first day of her kidnapping. She's worried that might be the reason for her fever."

"Gideon?" Kostya asked.

"I'll do research," Gideon replied. "Nolan won't be able to talk for a while."

"Shit," Brax answered. "How bad is it?"

There was a long pause. Finally, Kostya answered. "It's not good."

"I'll get back to you as soon as I can," Gideon said.

Brax looked down at Jenny. "They're researching the problem."

"You said 'how bad is it'. They must know something."

"They were talking about my teammate in the other

SUV behind us. He's been shot. He's alive, but Nolan is working on him."

"Shouldn't you be helping Nolan?" she asked. "I'm fine. I'm just sleepy."

Brax gave a tight grin. "Honey, they have all the men they need over there. I'm right where I want to be. As for you ingesting animal blood, one of my teammates is researching that, and he'll call back." He glanced up at the bag hanging from a hook. It was half empty. "You've got a full dose of medicine in you and some saline."

Jenny relaxed. At least she might know soon what was going on. Now that she was finally out of the hut, there wasn't a chance in hell she was going to let herself die.

"What the fuck? Stop that! It hurts!"

Brax winced, then smiled. At least she wasn't sounding all weak and pleading. If she had the strength, he'd bet his coveted first edition, signed copy of *Stranger in a Strange Land* by Robert Heinlein that Jenny would have taken a swing at him.

"Honey, I'm sorry it hurts. I'm doing something called percussion. I'm just tapping on your lower back so it will break up the mucus in your lungs."

"Well, fucking stop it, you asshole. I thought you were one of the good guys." She tried to shrug his hand off her back, and as soon as she did, she started to cough. The loud, deep, grating coughs made him wince. The coughs had to hurt, but they were just the thing she needed to do to help her get up the mucus.

The SUV started slipping and sliding as Ryker tried to maintain control as he stopped the vehicle. "We've got a problem," Ryker said into his mic from the front seat. "There's a couple of trees down, and they've dammed up the water. They've damn near created a lake."

9

"Everybody but Nolan and Brax, get out. You two stay with our wounded. I want this cleared ASAP." Ryker was out of his driver's side door before Kostya even finished giving his direction. *Dammit.* Kostya even had Gideon out there clearing the way, instead of continuing to gather intel. Brax sure would have liked to know how far away they were from Silchari. Even with the dry t-shirt, and the two of them sharing his poncho, Jenny's slight frame was racked with chills, despite her skin being hotter than hell.

Nolan had left his thermometer, and the last time Brax had checked, her fever was up to one-hundred-and three point six. Not good. He would have thought with the antibiotics it would have gone down.

He looked at the water bottle in his hands and opened the cap. He felt powerless. But dammit, he had no other option, he had to get her to drink. What the fuck else was there to do?

"Nolan," he tapped his mic. "Her fever's going up. When are the antibiotics going to start working, man?"

"It's only been thirty-five minutes. Give it time."

"Does she have that much time? Either she's coughing or groaning in pain."

"Brax, those are good things. That means she's still awake, right?"

He raked his fingers through his hair. "I guess. But still, is it going to be enough?"

"Even with the rain, and having to move the trees, we should be able to get to Chattogram by nightfall."

He heard his friend's answer, but he couldn't feel it in his gut. Not when he looked down at the wan features of the woman in his arms. They had to save her. She couldn't die, not after all of this. She just couldn't.

"There has to be something else I can be doing besides tapping on her back and waking her up to drink water."

"She's chilled, right?" Nolan asked.

"She's shivering. I know it's the fever, because her body is hot as fuck."

"You got to get her temperature down. Take off her clothes and wipe her down with cold water. Even if she wakes up and tells you to stop, keep doing it. That should help."

Now for the question he didn't want to ask. "How's Jase?"

"I've already given him blood. Linc's his blood type, and you know Gideon's O negative."

Brax nodded to himself. "Is that helping?"

"He's stabilizing."

"Did it hit his bone?"

"Yeah," Nolan answered.

That was it. Just the one-word answer.

"Brax, right now I'm focusing on keeping him in good enough shape for surgery. Yeah?"

"Gotcha."

Brax understood what Nolan was saying. This was no time worrying about Jase's future, they needed to take one bite of the elephant at a time. Anyway, he had Jenny to worry about. He still had her held close under his poncho with him, trying to share his body heat so that she wouldn't be shivering as much. The idea of forcing cold water on her was anathema, but it had to be done.

He carefully moved her, so that she was laying down on the tarp, then grabbed two of the empty water bottles and sheared off the tops with his knife. He opened the tailgate of the SUV and saw her violently shiver. He filled up the two water bottles with rain, then closed the door. They really didn't need the vehicle filled with water.

He looked at Jenny dispassionately and took off her boots first. It was a challenge that finally required him to just cut through her mud-caked shoelaces. As he peeled off her socks, he could see how swollen her feet were. It didn't look like infection had set in, which was a good thing. Then he took off her cargo pants. They easily slipped off since they were so large on her. He would bet anything she'd lost weight since being captured. He left her panties on. Then he pulled off her sweat-soaked shirt.

He poured some of the water directly onto her sternum, and she cried out. He forced himself to ignore her, as he used the soft shirt to stroke the cold water all along her torso, her breasts, up and down her arms, along her sides, around her neck, then across her brow.

Jenny's teeth were chattering and at one point, she attempted to grab his hand.

"Stop," she slurred the word.

"I can't. We need to get your fever down."

"C-c-cold."

"I know you are, Jenny. But this will help you get better. Trust me."

He poured water along her concave belly, then smoothed it down her hips above her panties, then down her thighs, along her knees and calves, then back up again. She struggled against him. She whimpered, and he had to steel himself against her obvious distress.

For long minutes he continued, then he pulled her back up into his arms, as if he were holding a baby over his shoulder and began smoothing the cold water over her back.

"Please, stop," she whispered into his ear. "Please."

Had he ever had a harder mission?

Finally, he laid her back down on top of the cold tarp and got the forehead thermometer. One-hundred-and-two point six. Her fever had reduced by a point, but now silent tears slipped down each side of her face, down to her temples and mixing in with her mud-caked hair.

Jenny looked nothing like the woman he had seen in the picture. Nothing. Until those first few minutes when she had opened her eyes and shown her fighting spirit. What had they done to her? How had they hurt her? The fact that she had shown that fighting spirit instead of the hollow-eyed, empty look of women they had rescued in the past gave him hope she hadn't been violated.

"Is there any rope or chains in the SUVs?" Kostya asked over the comm. "Two of these trees are still connected to the trunks and roots. We need more power."

Brax covered Jenny with his poncho, then moved her so that she was pushed up against the two front seats and prayed that there was some concealed storage. When he spotted it, his heart sank. Looking at the lid, he figured it could house a couple of grenades and maybe, just maybe, a sniper rifle. Sure as hell not an automatic rifle. They were shit out of luck. He opened it up anyway, and his eyes bugged out of his head.

"Kostya, the God of War is on our side today. I'm counting three, no make that four, tow straps in here. Depending on the size of the trees, the Land Cruiser should have enough torque to move them. If not, we can attach them to the van."

Before he was done talking, Kostya was lifting up the tailgate. He actually saw a grin on his lieutenant's face.

"You done good," he said as he grabbed the first strap and connected it to the hook on the tow hitch and started running with the others toward the trees. Ryker ran up to the tailgate. He stopped for a moment.

"How's she doing?"

"Better. The fever's come down a bit."

"Good."

He ran to get into the driver's seat. Brax closed the compartment, then spread out the tarp and pulled Jenny back into a prone position. She was out cold again, and she was shivering.

Dammit!

He took her temperature. It had gone back up to one-hundred and three.

"Start moving, Ryker. Slowly," Kostya commanded over the comm.

Brax shifted Jenny so she was sitting up, then cupped her cheek. "Jenny. I need you to wake up."

Her eyelashes fluttered. Her long eyelashes.

He bent closer. "Jenny, honey. You need to wake up and drink some water."

"Don't wanna," she slurred.

Good enough. He put the water bottle to her mouth and poured a trickle in. She shook her head and opened her eyes.

"I said no." She was still slurring her words, but she said them with more force.

"You don't have a choice. You want to get better, don't you? You want to beat those bastards and show them how tough you are. Drink the water and get well."

Her green eyes were glassy, but they still assessed him.

"Fine."

He slowly tipped the bottle, and she took sip after sip until she gagged and turned her head away. "Enough."

Her gagging precipitated a bout of coughing. It was a long one. She hadn't coughed for at least fifteen minutes. He saw her tears as her weak arm slid slowly up to cradle her ribs. Brax carefully rolled her over so that she could rid herself of the sputum. When she was done, she tried to turn back, and he helped her.

"I hate this so much. It hurts, and I hate that you're seeing me like this."

"Do you know how many recruits I've had to clean up after they've puked during BUD/S? Do you know how many times we've been in a jungle like this one and one or two of us are almost incapacitated with the shits? Jenny, you having to spit up some gunk from your lungs is a walk in the park."

"BUD/S?"

Good, she was tracking with him. That meant she was better, right?

"BUD/S stands for Basic Underwater Demolition SEALs. It's the training every recruit has to go through to become a SEAL. In my class, only a quarter of us made it through."

She looked at him with that glassy-eyed stare, and he thought he lost her.

"Why did so many quit?" she finally asked.

The SUV suddenly jerked and she let out a quick scream.

"It's okay," Ryker said from the front seat. "We just started pulling some trees out of the way. Everything's good. I want to hear more about BUD/S. And shame on you for not using the term diarrhea. You're going to go to hell for talking crass around a lady."

Jenny giggled.

"Ryker, mind your own business and concentrate on driving," Brax groused. He turned his attention to the woman in his arms. "Do you still—"

He was interrupted by another bout of her coughing. This seemed even worse than the last one. He felt so helpless. At least with some kind of injury, he could do something.

Bullshit.

Brax thought about how Nolan must be feeling in the van with Jase. Jase, who had lost so much blood that he needed two transfusions and the bullet had hit his femur. Brax's gut clenched. What was his teammate going to do if he ended up permanently injured?

Stop it!

One bite of the elephant at a time.

One step at a time.

He helped Jenny roll over so she could spit up in the towel. He did more percussion on her back to help her get up even more mucus. He kept the taps against the side where her ribs weren't either broken or bruised. Finally, she stopped. He looked down and saw blood on the towel. As he rolled her over, blood had dripped from her nose, over her mouth, and down her chin. He spoke into his mic.

"Nolan, she has a bloody nose again."

"Brax, I don't know what to tell you. Put a cold cloth at the bridge of her nose; that will help stop the bleed.

With everything else, she can't afford to be losing blood. What's her temp?"

Brax looked around and found the thermometer. "Same as last time. One-oh-three point six."

"Wash her down with cold water again."

Brax closed his eyes for a moment. "Will do."

He felt the SUV strain as it pulled the tree. "How we doing, Ryker?"

"It's not good. We're over three and half RPM. Three RPM should be our max."

"Kostya?" Ryker asked.

"The tree is moving. We're pushing it out of the way as you're moving it. It's working. This is the biggest tree. After this one, it will be easy."

Smart man, start with the biggest when the engine had the most power.

Brax moved and lifted the tailgate window, filling up the two water bottles he'd turned into cups. He moved back to Jenny and went back to the process of stroking the wet t-shirt over her body. Her shivering continued, but she never woke up to tell him to stop. At least that was something.

"Stop!" Kostya said firmly into the comm. "This tree is out of the way. We can move to the next." Brax heard Ryker's sigh of relief.

"How close?" Brax asked.

"We were at four RPM. I was afraid the tow hook might have sheared off," Ryker answered. He started backing up so that they could play the game again. Brax played the same game and wiped Jenny down. This time she did wake up, but she didn't plead for him to stop. He saw her close her lips so tight that they were rimmed with white.

"Almost done," he promised her.

She nodded, finally letting her teeth chatter, but still no words.

"Jenny, you with me?"

The truck jerked again.

"Kostya, how many trees?" he demanded to know.

"Just three. We're hoping when they're moved the water will disperse."

"How high is the water?"

"Don't ask," Kostya responded.

Fuck.

Stop it, Walker. Focus on the good. Nolan's got Jase stable. Jenny's fever has never exceeded one-oh-three point six and we'd found tow straps.

He looked down at Jenny. Her eyes were shut tight. "Jenny, you with me?"

She gave one sharp nod.

"Not good enough. I need to see those pretty green eyes."

"She has green eyes? Damn, I love a woman with green eyes," Ryker said from the front seat.

"Cut it out, or I'll tell Amy you were flirting with another woman," Brax called back.

Jenny opened one eye and her lip twitched.

She was here with him. He took the thermometer out and slid it across her forehead. One-oh-two point eight. He grinned. Definitely down. It was either the antibiotics working or the cold wipe-downs. He didn't give a damn what it was, just so long as it was working.

"Ryker, you can stop," Kostya said over the comm. "We're onto the last tree. Water's already dispersing. This is working."

Brax felt his shoulders relax. "Gideon, what's the ETA to Chattogram?"

"You mean Chattanooga?" Jase's voice came over the comm. Brax could barely hear him.

"Nolan, is he delirious?" Brax asked.

"Nah," Nolan said. "He's attempting to be funny. As usual, he's falling flat."

"Am not," Jase slurred. "Already flat... Can't fall."

Every single man on the team started chuckling with relief. It was clear that all of them had been scared to death about Jase.

Smiling, Brax looked down at Jenny and saw that her nose was bleeding again.

10

The plan had been to extract and take Ms. Rivers into India so that they could fly home to the States from there. There wasn't a chance in hell that was going to work considering her condition, not to mention Jase's. The way Brax figured it, as soon as the two of them could be stabilized, the US Embassy would insist that they be flown out to the military hospital in Landstuhl, Germany.

Getting the hell out of Silchari and heading to Chattogram took a lot more time than they would have liked. There was no way that they could traverse the roads, if they could be called roads, from Silchari to Kaptai Lake at any kind of decent speed, so they didn't get there until the middle of the night, and the rain sure as hell didn't help.

It was there that the roads evened out a little. Gideon found them a bridge over the many islands in the Kaptai river, so they finally ended up on the East side of Kaptai Lake and on an interstate.

"Ryker, no speeding. The last thing we need is to be pulled over," Kostya said over the comm.

"How much longer?" Ryker asked.

"Two hours," Gideon answered.

"How are our patients?"

Brax didn't answer, and he noticed Nolan didn't either.

"I'm speeding," Ryker said decisively.

Kostya didn't reply.

Brax looked down at Jenny, who hadn't roused since the last time he had her talking. At least her nose bleed had stopped. The saline bag was empty. It was time for more water. He cupped her cheek. He'd cleaned her up earlier, and he noticed how soft her skin was despite her ordeal. "Jenny, it's me, Brax. Can you wake up for me?"

This time, her eyelashes didn't even flutter.

He hitched her up higher on his knee, then shook her shoulder. "Jenny. I need you to wake up for me. It's time to drink some water."

Still nothing.

He knew she was still with him, because of the bouts of coughing she did in her sleep, and because he'd kept his thumb on her pulse almost the entire time they'd been driving.

He moved his knee so that she was cradled in his embrace, and now sitting up.

"Uh-uh. Sleep." Somehow, he understood her words.

"Nope, no sleep for the wicked," he teased. "There's

a full day of work ahead for you. First thing on your plate is to drink some water."

"Don' wanna."

He adored that petulant tone.

"Did you notice you didn't cough?"

"Big deal. Don't wanna drink water." Her voice sounded stronger

"No choice, honey." Brax lifted the water bottle to her lips and dribbled some water against her closed lips. Finally, he gave up.

"Okay, what do you want?"

She opened her eyes and frowned. "Wan peash smoothie."

"If you drink some water, you'll get a peach smoothie. Is it a deal?"

"Kay."

"You're going to hell," Ryker whispered from the front.

After ten minutes, he got an entire bottle of water into Jenny and felt like he had just come in first at target practice.

She went limp in his arms. He thought she'd passed out again. He leaned down and whispered in her ear. "You with me?"

"Where's peash smoothie?" she slurred.

"Soon."

"Now."

Ryker was right, I'm going to hell.

"I'll get you a peach smoothie soon, honey. Soon. First, we have to get you well."

Her eyes opened and this close he could see a little

bit of blue mixed with the green. "You rescued me, right?"

"Me and a lot of others. We all rescued you."

"Thank you. Thank them all."

"I will. Sleep now."

BEFORE THEY EVEN REACHED THE city limits of Chattogram, Gideon started talking.

"Ryker, this is it. Pull off 163 and take a right onto Oxygen Kuwaish Road."

"How far am I going?"

"In a mile, on your right, is going to be Evercare Hospital. It'll be a good place to start getting them care and stabilized before we get Jase on a flight to Germany for surgery."

"What do you mean, Jase?" Brax interrupted. "What about Jenny?"

"Spoke to the Embassy. Since she's not military, they want her to go straight to America after she's stabilized. It's going to be tough going for her, though."

"What are you talking about?"

"It got out that she'd been kidnapped, and that her company screwed her over. It's made national news. Everybody and their brother are going to want to interview her."

Brax swallowed down bile. That was the last thing Jenny needed. "That's all the more reason to take her to the American military hospital in Germany."

"Can't. The embassy is insisting that getting her

back to the States and proving that she is well is their number one priority."

"How's Jase doing?" Ryker interrupted.

That gave Brax a moment to cool down and take Jenny's temperature for the umpteenth time. It was one-oh-three point eight.

Dammit.

"I gave him something for the pain," Nolan answered Ryker. "He's out. From what I can tell there are no fragments in his leg, and if that's the case I just want them to put him in a soft cast so they can operate on him in Landstuhl."

The men on the comm all grunted in agreement.

It was decided that Kostya, Linc, Ryker, Gideon and Mateo would drive over the Indian border to Kolkata, and fly to Germany from there. In the meantime, Nolan would stay with Jase and Brax would stay with Jenny when they checked into the hospital.

Brax continued to hold Jenny in his arms as he watched Jase get immediate attention in the emergency room and rushed back through the double doors.

Nolan got the attention of one of the doctors who had assessed Jase and practically dragged him over to where Brax was standing with Jenny. The doctor took one look at Jenny and said, "She's not a priority."

"She absolutely is a priority," Brax growled. "She's severely dehydrated. She has pneumonia. Her temperature is over one-hundred and four degrees, and she has at least one broken rib."

The doctor looked around the overflowing emergency room and hesitated. Then he slipped his stethoscope from around his neck and listened to Jenny's lungs. He listened for maybe fifteen seconds before she started coughing. Deep racking coughs that had her weak arm creeping up her body to clutch at her side where her ribs were hurting.

The doctor looked up at Brax, and that was when Brax noticed he looked like a kid, despite his air of authority. "You're right. We need to get her seen," the doctor said. "Bring her back."

Nolan followed Brax as he pushed through the double doors. Brax knew he needed to explain what needed to be done with Jase. None of the team wanted Jase's surgery to be done here. He needed to be operated on at the military hospital in Germany. Where were the Embassy guys?

Brax laid Jenny down carefully on one of the beds in the ER, and a different doctor came over to assess her. While he examined her IV, he tried to get Jenny to answer questions, but it was no use, she was too out of it to answer, so Brax did.

The nurse was hooking the tubing to the IV and taking her temperature, blood pressure, pulse and oxygen levels.

"She seems severely malnourished, dehydrated besides having pneumonia. How did she get in this state?"

"Her name is Jenny Rivers. She was kidnapped

twenty-eight days ago. I don't know how much she was fed, but by the looks of her, not much."

"Kidnapped?" The whites of the doctor's eyes showed.

"Yes. Some of my friends and I rescued her yesterday. I'm convinced that at least one of her ribs is broken. I don't know what kind of abuse she has been through."

The doctor nodded. "We'll need to get x-rays of her lungs and ribs after we get her fever down."

"Her nose has been bleeding," Brax told him.

The doctor pulled a scope off the wall and looked up Jenny's nose. "There is a great deal of dried mud inside her nose, irritating the vessels. That and dehydration is what causes the bleeding. It's nothing to worry about. Her fever is what concerns me the most." He turned to the nurse. "Begin the protocols to reduce her fever and get a culture."

The nurse nodded.

The doctor turned to Brax. "I'll need you to wait in the waiting room."

"That's not going to happen. Ms. Rivers is an American citizen who was targeted by mercenaries. As soon as she is stable, the American Embassy is going to want to fly her to the States. It is my job to ensure her safety. I need to stay close to her, even while she is being treated in the hospital."

The doctor gave him a long look. "All right. But don't get in our way, otherwise I'll call security."

Brax held back a grin. Yeah, like security was going

to stop him from doing any damn thing he wanted to do.

He stayed in the emergency room bay as he watched them pump her full of fluids. He continued to ask what they were doing. Kostya called at one point.

"Yeah?"

"I got a hold of the Embassy there in Bangladesh. They're sending a representative tomorrow to talk to Ms. Rivers. They're going to want to ask her questions."

"Good luck with that. She's out of it."

"Washington has informed the Embassy what our involvement was. They're not happy, but they know. So, you can give them a rundown."

"Where are you?"

"We're almost to Dhaka. We still need to lie low until we get to India. I'm going to call Nolan next and tell him what we have set up to get Jase to Germany."

"That's going to happen?"

"Of course it is." Brax could hear the smile in his leader's voice.

BRAX WAS SITTING in Jenny's private room when the Embassy official came in to interview her. He immediately disliked him. Jenny was still pretty much out of it. She was gaunt, glassy-eyed and clearly in pain despite the pain meds.

"Hello, Ms. Rivers," the young American said. "I'm Peter Meyer. I work at the American Embassy here in

Bangladesh. I am very sorry about the situation you found yourself in."

Jenny's eyes opened just enough so that Brax could see a little bit of green.

"Situation?" she whispered.

Brax's blood was boiling at numb-nuts using that word to diminish Jenny's kidnapping.

"Yes. We realize the circumstances were difficult for you, and we want to know what happened from your point-of-view so that we can understand who perpetrated this offense and provide the Bangladeshi government with the pertinent facts."

"Are you out of your mind?" Brax rose from his chair, throwing the book he was reading on the floor. "What are you talking about, her circumstances? She was fucking kidnapped and kept in a shack without a proper roof and a bucket for a toilet for three weeks. Look at her, she was barely fed, and she's lucky to be alive."

The little pissant wasn't cowering which pissed Brax off even more. He looked at Brax like he was a bug that needed to be brushed off.

"Be that as it may, my job is to ensure our relationship with Bangladesh remains as harmonious as possible. Blowing things out of proportion is not going to help."

"Fuck that! Fuck harmonious! Look at her!"

"You're one of the military men who retrieved her, is that correct?"

"Yes. I'm one of the members of the SEAL team that went in and *rescued* her, that's correct."

This guy needs a personality adjustment and I'm just the man to give it to him.

"You're really not needed at this point. It was my understanding that you and your team were departing to India and then flying home. You should have done the same."

"And leave her to a vulture like you? I don't think so. Here's how it's going to go. Any questions you have, you ask me."

"Brax." Jenny's voice was barely a whisper.

"Just rest, Jenny. Leave this to me."

"Brax," Jenny said in a hoarse voice.

Brax turned to Jenny and gave her a tight smile. "Jenny, I promise. I've got this." Then he turned back to the Embassy creep. "Now listen to me—"

"Brax," Jenny's voice was sharp, then she began to cough.

"Now look what you've done," Brax said as he moved to Jenny. As he lifted a cup with a straw in it to her mouth, she attempted to shove it away, but she was still too weak.

When she finally stopped coughing, she glared up at Brax. "I can speak for myself."

He winced at the grating sound of her voice.

"I'm helping."

She looked up at him. Her eyes were clearer than he'd ever seen them. "No, you're making this take longer."

"I don't want you upset," he finally whispered.

Then she smiled at him and his heart melted.

"Thank you, Brax. Thank you for taking care of me, but I can handle this part." She reached out her hand for the cup of water and he held it to her lips. She grasped his wrist with her free hand and took a long sip. When she was done, it seemed like she caressed his skin as he took the cup away.

God, I need to get a grip.

"What was your name again?" Jenny asked the embassy guy.

"Peter Meyer. I work in the Embassy's Regional Security Office. I need to find out everything that went on when you disappeared."

Jenny shifted, and Brax saw she was trying to sit up.

"Let me help you."

He'd noted that the bed didn't have an automatic lift, so he helped her up and fluffed the pillows behind her so that she could be more comfortable in a seated position.

"What do you need to know about my 'situation'?"

Meyer winced. "You need to understand. Now that you have been found safe, it is our hope not to escalate this incident here in Bangladesh. We realize that it has already generated a lot of interest in the US."

Jenny leaned forward. "What are you talking about?"

"The political situation in Bangladesh is already complex enough without the US getting thrown into the mix. But if you were targeted by either of the two main political parties, the Awami League or the BNP, then I need to know."

"I think, to begin with, they were trying to make me think that they were members of Awami, but they weren't. By the end of the first day, I knew they were just kidnappers out for a buck."

"How can you be so sure?" Meyer asked.

"I've lived in Bangladesh for two years. My job is public affairs for New Era Cyber Tech in Dhaka and that means I've had to talk to..." She took a deep breath and motioned for Brax to give her more water. When she was done drinking, she continued. "In my job, I've had to talk to many people in public arenas, including politicians, academics, bureaucrats, CEOs and decision makers here in Bangladesh. I've run across members of the Awami League and the Bangladesh National Party. But they were completely unlike the people who kidnapped me. Those people were filth."

Brax watched as Meyer cringed.

"But I want to know what you meant about this being of public interest in the United States?"

Meyer looked over at Brax and Brax shrugged. This was all Meyer's problem; he was the one who brought it up.

"Two of your colleagues who worked with you here in Dhaka brought it to the press that you had been kidnapped, after they determined that New Era Cyber Tech was not paying the ransom. It's made quite a stir in the media."

Jenny turned to look at Brax, and he nodded. She closed her eyes and rested her head against the pillows. Then she looked back at Brax. "What does that mean for me?"

"I'm thinking a big payout from your company, so you don't sue their ass off."

She gave him a weak grin.

"Brax, I can't handle reporters when I get home."

After hearing her sound so strong, he hated hearing her sound defeated.

Brax had wheedled Jenny's biography from Gideon, and learned that she was from Wyoming and both of her parents were dead. Her social media accounts were practically non-existent.

"We can arrange for you to stay in a hotel for a couple of weeks," Meyer said.

She squinted at the security officer. "Why would you do that?"

"It's in everybody's best interest for this story to die down," he answered.

Brax liked how she looked over at him for guidance. "You used to live in Chesapeake, Virginia, before you took this job, right?" Brax asked.

She nodded. "I put everything into a storage unit. Part of my company package is that they would give me a lump sum bonus for a down payment on a house when I finished this assignment since I was giving up my home. Or I could just pocket the money."

"Grab a hotel in Chesapeake, since you know the area. My team and I are in Virginia Beach, so we can help if things get out of hand."

"I don't think that's protocol," Meyer interrupted.

"Thought you wanted to keep things on the downlow." Brax raised his eyebrow at Meyer.

"Well, yes," the man sputtered.

"Can you think of many other people better able to keep things under wraps than a team of Navy SEALs?"

Peter Meyer sighed.

Jenny gave him a grateful smile.

11

Jenny flipped on the television for the fourth time in as many minutes, then turned it off again. The idea of watching a sitcom, the news, or a reality TV show held no appeal. She looked down at her cell phone and grimaced. Peter Meyer had gotten her a new one that had her number, contacts, and everything else downloaded from her cloud. The last time she'd turned it on, her voicemail had been full of messages from people from her company, but mostly calls from reporters.

"Dammit!"

She got off the couch, went over to the window, and looked outside. Still raining. Why was it that, after leaving a monsoon, she came home to rain? At least she was feeling better. The week in the hospital made a difference. She was still wearing a bandage around her ribs and coughing a lot, but she was beginning to feel human.

Maybe that was part of the problem. She felt better,

but here she was hiding out near the Norfolk airport, going stir-crazy.

I need to get a plan together.

She went over to the hotel phone and picked up the notepad with Brax and Peter's numbers written down on it. The final two days she'd been in the hospital, Brax had come to visit. He'd mumbled something about not being able to come sooner because of debriefings and red tape. It had scared her how grateful she'd been to see him. It wasn't like her. Since her mom's death she prided herself on not relying on anyone.

For the nineteen days she'd been cooped up here at beige central, which was how she'd come to think of her small hotel suite, his morning and evening calls were the highlight of her days. It was crazy. She didn't even really know the man.

"Try pulling your other leg, Rivers. Now you know a lot about the man, and he knows a lot about you."

At least he doesn't know I talk to myself.

Besides the phone, Peter got her a tablet with all the bells and whistles. So far, she'd only used it to run searches on the internet about herself. She needed to stop it. Talk about something that was freaking her out. Why would people care so much about her? She was a nobody, and she liked it that way.

I need to get out of here. I need to do something!

She plopped back down on the sofa and hissed as the jerky movement sliced pain up her side. Apparently, her two ribs would take a few more weeks to heal.

She didn't need to look at the paper when she picked up the hotel phone to call Brax; she'd memorized his number.

"Jenny?"

She looked at the receiver, stunned he'd picked up on the first ring.

"Uhm, hi."

"Hi. Are you all right?"

She couldn't believe the concern in his voice. It was weird.

"Yeah, I'm fine. I'm sorry to bother you. I know you'll call tonight. I just should have waited. Ignore me. I'll talk to you later. Bye."

"Wait! Don't hang up. Jenny, it's not a problem. I told you to call anytime. What's going on?"

She snorted out a laugh. "What could possibly be going on inside these beige walls? It's so boring, I actually watched part of a golf game."

Brax let out a laugh. Had she ever really heard him laugh before? She couldn't remember.

"Golf, huh? That's pretty bored."

"Tell me about it. Why is it that CNN still has me on one of their new stories? It's been almost three weeks since I've been home. It's ridiculous. I turned on my phone yesterday and considered clearing out my messages, but then my phone rang. It was a reporter. Brax, I'd only had my phone on for three minutes. What are the odds?"

"It's because you haven't given an interview, and the public is really pissed at Cyber Tech for hanging you out to dry. You've read that part, haven't you?"

Jenny couldn't stop the evil smile that crept across her face. "Yeah. Serves them right. I bet Roy is about to have a heart attack."

"Who's Roy?"

"He's the Vice President in charge of Public Relations for all of New Era Cyber Tech. It's his job to make sure the company's reputation is always pristine. I don't know how he's going to clean up this steaming pile."

"Of dog shit?" Brax asked. "Yeah, I don't think he can."

"I feel like I'll never be able to leave this hotel room, and I'm sick of club sandwiches. I need fresh air."

"Why don't I come and rescue you?"

"Aren't you sick of rescuing me?"

"I shouldn't have used that phrase. Jenny, I would love to spend some time with you when you're feeling well. I'll even bring over some stuff so you won't be recognized."

Huh?

"Okaaay."

"Trust me?"

Now that was an easy answer. "Always."

WHEN BRAX SLIPPED his phone into his back pocket, he realized his palms were actually damp. *What the hell?*

Oh yeah. Jenny.

He'd thought about her every day since she'd been released from the hospital, and the morning and evening phone calls weren't enough to soothe his need to see her. But the idea of doing anything more than checking up on her via telephone had been a bridge too far. Getting involved with someone who was still recovering from being a captive wasn't the best idea.

He jogged to his bedroom and Faith followed him. He pulled on his boots while his dog planted her ass down in front of him. He could see her excitement.

"Nope, I'm not taking you out, girl. We've already gone out twice today. This time I'm going out by myself."

Woof.

He shook his head. "Not this time."

Woof. Woof.

"If you understand me this well, why in the hell don't you obey me when I say fetch?"

Faith just stared at him.

"Yep, you're a female all right."

Woof.

Shit. Brax knew when he had been reprimanded for a sexist comment.

He got up, went to his coat closet, and pulled out a U of V Cavaliers hoodie that CiCi had left a couple of months ago, along with one of his good, broken-in ball caps. Then he grabbed his keys from the dusty fruit bowl on his kitchen counter and headed out to his truck.

When he got to the Hyatt near the Norfolk Airport, he took the ticket to park his car, then walked past reception and hit the bank of elevators. He knew which room Jenny was in. He'd made it his business. She answered the door with a bright smile, but he frowned.

"Did you look through the peephole?"

"Of course I did. After Bangladesh, I'm big-time security conscious."

He looked around the room and saw that one of the stuffed chairs that should be close to the sofa, was next to the door.

Damn.

"What's that?" She tilted her head toward the hoodie and ball cap in his hand.

"This is your disguise." He handed it over to her.

"A Cav hoodie? No way. I'm Tar Heels all the way. I can't wear that."

He laughed. "So sorry. Tar Heels weren't allowed in my household. How'd you become a Duke fan? I thought you went to school in Colorado, not North Carolina."

"I did. But my roommate's brother went to Duke and played wide receiver. It was mandatory I become a fan."

"Even when you lived in Virginia for the last six years?"

"I've only actually lived here for about a year total. Other than that, I took assignments all over the country and the world."

"Well, you're going to have to wear the hoodie and the ball cap if you want to escape for a bit."

She rolled her eyes. "Fine. But I'm doing this under protest."

"So noted." He tried not to laugh at her sass. He

knew she was trying to make him think that she had moved past her captivity, but from her daily phone calls, he knew she hadn't. But he was going to let her take the lead...for now.

He watched as she started walking back to her bedroom. "Dress warm. It's cold outside," he called after her.

"Gotcha." She waved over her shoulder at him.

As soon as the door was closed, he pushed at the chair. It was heavier than it looked, and she still looked like a strong wind would blow her over. It told him just how scared she still was. The woman was a good actress. He needed to remember that.

She came out of the bedroom smiling, and he took a good look at her. Skinny jeans, sneakers, the hoodie and the ballcap.

"Do you have a jacket?"

She shook her head.

"I'd say a shopping trip is in order."

Jenny's smile changed to a grimace. "Peter got me my ID, but I'm having trouble with my bank. They want to send my debit and credit cards to my old address, which I moved out of a year and a half ago."

"How did you do your banking while you were in Bangladesh?"

"All paperless."

"Makes sense. And I take it they won't send your replacement cards here? To a hotel, I mean."

"Nope."

"After we get you a jacket, then we can go to your bank. Hopefully, somebody high enough will understand your circumstances. After all, you've made national news."

"Yay me, something positive about having so many reporters crawling up my butt. As for the jacket, we need to do that after I get my money."

"Just let me spot you some upfront."

"Uh-uh. What happens if we can't untangle it today? I don't want to owe you." Her mutinous expression reminded him of a cute four-year-old girl who didn't want to eat her Brussels sprouts. She was adorable. But he knew he would be handed his ass if he told her that. He tried for humor. "Jenny, you already owe me for keeping you alive, what's the problem with owing me money for a week or two?"

Her lips twitched. "Yeah, I really do. I tell you what, the next time you get kidnapped I'll insist on coming along with your team and help rescue you, how about that?"

Brax gave a mock shudder. "How about you promise not to go along? That would be a real favor. I would like to live."

"Picky little princess, aren't you?"

Her smile brought sunshine into the beige room and Brax couldn't help but laugh. "Now you know my baby sister's nickname for me, PLP."

"Baby sister? What's her name? What's she like?"

"Let's get out of here and get on the road, and I'll tell you about CiCi. You two would really get along."

"Do you think so?"

Brax caught a bit of longing in her voice. It was funny that she'd never mentioned any visitors since staying at the hotel. He knew she was steering clear of NECT employees, but where were her other friends? He knew her parents were dead, and she'd been an only child, but still, didn't she have friends? He'd have to dig a little.

"I *know* you and CiCi would hit it off. I'd bring her along to shop, but with her along, we'd never make it to the bank before it closes."

"She's a shopper?"

"If she could make a career out of it, she would." He hit the button for the elevator, and soon they were on the way to his truck. When he got the passenger door open, she stared up at the seat. She was a tiny little thing. "Do you need help getting in?"

"If you could explain how I'm supposed to get in without a step ladder, I'd sure appreciate it."

"Step up on the running board, then grab this handle up here, and then you can step into the wheel well and swing onto the seat."

He watched with appreciation as she gracefully entered his truck, then looked down at him. "Was it really necessary to buy such a large truck?"

"Absolutely. The bigger, the better." He closed her door, then ran around to get into the driver's side and start his baby up. He looked over at her, he could see that she was favoring her ribs a little. No matter how graceful she wanted to be, he'd help her up next time.

"At least you haven't got those enormous tires and that huge rack of lights on the top. If you did, I might have had to cancel the shopping trip."

"Just the shopping trip?"

She gave him a quick sideways glance. "I'd suck it up for the bank trip."

Brax laughed at her put-upon voice.

"What's your bank? We can do that on the way to the mall."

She told him the national bank, and where the branch was.

"Great. Then we're a go."

12

After talking to the branch manager for a half hour, Jenny was ready to tear her hair out. She looked over her shoulder to where Brax was sitting. She needed to see a friendly face for a moment. Someone who would provide encouragement that she could and would get this mess sorted out.

She turned back to the banker.

"Mr. Anderson, I no longer live there, and currently I don't have a permanent address."

"The address on your driver's license shows the address we have on file. That's where we are obligated to send your documents."

"Why not just have them sent to this branch and allow me to pick them up?"

"That's not our policy."

He looked over her shoulder. "Excuse me? Who are you?"

"I'm Ms. Rivers' friend. I'm Chief Petty Officer

Braxton Walker with the United States Navy, out of Little Creek."

Jenny watched as Mr. Anderson sat up a little straighter. Mr. Anderson was an older gentleman who was obviously impressed with Brax. Jenny would bet money it was the Little Creek part. She'd made it her business to learn about Navy SEALs when she got out of the hospital. Little Creek, Virginia was where they were all stationed on the East Coast. Apparently, everybody in Virginia knew that except for her. That's why Mr. Anderson was looking so impressed. She scooched her chair so that she could see both Brax and Mr. Anderson at the same time.

"Thank you for your service, young man," Mr. Anderson said. "But Ms. Rivers and I are having a private conversation, Chief Walker."

"She and I are friends. Are you aware of the circumstances regarding why she needed an all-new ID, credit cards and everything else you can think of?"

Anderson shook his head.

Brax looked down at Jenny and gave her a put-upon look. "Jenny, you should have told him." Brax took out his phone from his back pocket. He started scrolling, then handed his phone to the banker.

"This is Jenny."

"She's the woman—" he looked up at Brax. "Pardon me," Anderson said as he looked back at Jenny. "You're the woman who was kidnapped?"

Jenny nodded.

"She was held in captivity for over three weeks in Bangladesh. She was lucky to have survived. It was because of her guts and determination that she stayed alive."

"And being rescued, let's not forget that," Jenny said quietly.

Brax waved his hand.

"Ms. Rivers went through hell. What can you do to help her get into her accounts?"

"This is all highly irregular," Anderson started. "But you're right. Under these circumstances we need to make an exception." He looked back at Jenny. "You can make a cash withdrawal today with the ID that you do have, and I'll have your cards sent to this branch for you to pick up. Does that meet with your approval?"

She nodded, unsure who to thank, the banker or Brax.

AT LEAST JENNY hadn't given him a ration of shit when they left the bank. He'd been sure that was going to come his way after he butted in. But, no. Jenny surprised him once again. Instead, right there in the bank parking lot, she'd hugged him. She'd been positively giddy at the idea of having access to her money again.

Hell, Brax was giddy too, after that hug.

Down, boy. She's just been through hell. Don't take advantage.

As soon as they walked into the busy mall, Brax could see that Jenny wasn't doing well. Her face turned pale and there was a fine sheen of perspiration on her forehead.

"Are you doing, okay? We can buy you a coat online."

"We are not buying my coat online. That's blasphemous." He appreciated her strong voice, even though her wide eyes and dilated pupils told a much different story.

"Seriously Jenny, we can leave."

She stopped, forcing him to stop, too. She looked up at him. "I love shopping. A mall is my jam. I haven't been to a mall in America for over two years. I'm having a blast. Now stop talking about leaving."

"Wanna hold my hand?" he asked as he held it out.

She immediately grabbed hold. Her grip was as tight as a bowline knot.

If he had to guess, she was five minutes away from a panic attack, but this woman had guts, there was no two ways about it. "Which store do you want to hit first?"

"Dillard's."

Great, CiCi's favorite store. You had to pass the perfume counter to get in, and he always ended up getting sprayed with perfume. It was a guarantee. It even happened when he'd been a kid and had gone to the mall with his mom.

Brax shut that thought down quick and looked down at Jenny. *Yeah, focus on Jenny, that's the ticket.* Such pretty brown hair, all mixed with deep red strands and shimmering gold.

"There's a directory kiosk," Jenny pointed with her left hand.

Brax guided her over to the sign, and saw that Dillard's was on the opposite side of the mall.

Fuck.

"Do you feel like taking a walk outside?" he asked. "I could do with some more fresh air, and I'm thinking after being cooped up in the hotel for so long, you might like to walk around the mall, instead of plowing through the easy way. Am I right?"

The look of relief on her face said it all. "You're right. I really do need fresh air. Especially some crisp fall air, instead of the hot and humid air of Bangladesh. That sounds wonderful."

"I can only imagine." Brax muttered. He turned around and gave her hand a tug as he guided them to the exit. Being a big guy, most people gave them plenty of space, so by the time they got to the outside, Jenny was no longer grinding his knuckles together.

"Have you been here often?" Jenny asked, as they started their trek.

"God no. Malls are *not* my jam. I asked my sister where to go. She said this would have a variety that would be good. She'd know."

"It's been so long since I'd been home that I just couldn't think of anything. It's like my mind is mush."

"Cut yourself some slack. You've been through a trauma. You're probably going to have nightmares and flashbacks and lots of other issues as you process things. Remembering different malls isn't high on your brain's list of priorities. How's it going with your psychologist?"

"Huh?"

"The psychologist that Meyer set you up with after your debrief."

"Oh yeah. I blew that off."

They were still holding hands so Brax was frustrated he couldn't get a good look of her face. "What do you mean, you blew it off?"

"I went into counseling a couple of times when I was in college. It didn't do any good. Obviously, I'm not meant for that kind of thing."

Brax saw an empty bench coming up, and he pulled her toward it. Before they sat down, he took off his leather jacket and put it around her shoulders. He liked the way she snuggled into his coat.

"Why are we stopping?"

"I need a moment to catch my breath," Brax lied.

"Yeah, I so believe that. You were the one who carried me through the forest, without breaking a sweat."

"Actually, that was Nolan. He knew that I have trouble even lifting my backpack," Brax teased.

She shifted sideways even further, then took her time looking him up and down. She spent a long time looking at his chest and shoulders. "Yep. You definitely look like a ten-pound-weakling. It's amazing you made it through Buddy training."

"BUD/S."

"Whatever."

He loved seeing the twinkle in her eye as he

realized *she'd* been teasing. Brax shook his head and laughed.

"I'm thinking we stopped so you could lecture me, am I right?" Jenny queried.

Brax leaned back on the bench, his arms stretching along the back. He crossed one ankle to his knee. "I have a policy never to lecture beautiful women."

He watched her blush.

"So why are we sitting here? Oh." She bit her lower lip. "I wasn't really having a panic attack, you know. I could have pushed through the crowd."

"Honey, I don't doubt that in the slightest. You're one of the strongest women I've ever met. You remind me a lot of some of the other ladies of Omega Sky."

"Huh?"

"The name of my Navy SEAL team is Omega Sky. You didn't get a chance to meet the other men on my team, but all of the ones who were on the mission to rescue you have paired up with incredible women. Some of them have faced horrifying and traumatic circumstances, but they've all come out the other side stronger. That's going to be you, too."

"Yeah, sure I am." Jenny rolled her eyes. "Brax, I have to shove a chair against the door of my hotel room every night, even after I put on the deadbolt. I'm not stronger, I'm a hot mess."

"That's why you need to see a psychologist. Hell, they have one on tap for all of us if we need one."

"Hmm-mm. And how many times have you been to the psychologist?"

"I'll admit it, I haven't, but I know men who have.

One guy I know needed a psychologist for a long time. He said it really helped."

"He talked about it?"

"Absolutely, he talked about it. He didn't want there to be a stigma about seeking out help. He's one of the best snipers in all the SEAL teams."

"Can I ask why he needed to go, or is that too personal?"

"PTSD, same as you."

"Do you really think that's what's going on with me?" she asked in a whisper. He saw the hope and fear on her face.

Brax moved his arm and cupped her cheek. He brushed his thumb against the soft skin of her jaw. "I'm not sure, but that's what I suspect. I would check in with a professional, and then let them give you the tools to handle it, if it is PTSD. Or if it is something else, they could help with that, too."

She grabbed his wrist and he thought she was going to push him away, but instead she kept his hand where it was. "I'm not sure if I agree with your diagnosis, Dr. Walker. If it was me having flashbacks, I wouldn't be panicked about being in a mall full of people. As a matter of fact, I should be happy to be there. It should only be small, confined places that would make me panic."

Brax nodded. "I see your point. But you admit there's something?"

She nodded.

He slipped his hand around and cupped the back of her neck. "Wanna talk about it?"

She looked down and her dark brown eyelashes fanned her cheeks. When she looked up her green eyes shimmered with tears. "I guess. I'd prefer to talk to you, than some shrink."

Brax sucked in a deep breath, stunned that she would feel that comfortable with him. His ultimate goal was to get her to see someone, but in the meantime he could still listen.

"Okay. Lay it on me."

"When we were inside the mall, all those people were talking, and coming at us. I felt like I was going to be knocked over at any second. And the noise. It was so loud. Even in my hotel room, I can't handle loud TV shows. I'm fine with those whispery nature documentaries where they talk about lions in their natural habitats."

"So, you lied when you said that you were bored watching golf. You actually like it because the commentators whisper. Got it."

"Maybe," she admitted.

"Having a panic attack is nothing to be ashamed of. You know that, don't you?"

She bowed her head, and he couldn't stand it. He touched her chin and tilted her head back up. "Seriously, after everything you've been through, you're amazing. Trust me. Do you think you would be up for talking to my sister and a couple of friends of mine? They've been through some trauma, too. If you don't want to talk to a shrink, maybe talking to others who have been through the fire could help you."

"Like the sniper?"

"I was actually thinking of my sister and two or three other women."

"Not your sister. Don't tell me she went through something like I did. I would hate that for her."

He moved his hand and stroked it down her arm until he could tangle his fingers with hers. She had such a kind heart. He hated all *she* had been through.

"When my sister was four years old, she was diagnosed with a rare kind of cancer. She was in and out of the hospital as a child until she was nine years old. It was at that point that they thought they had cured her, but the thing was, she went in for yearly scans, because apparently once you have cancer, you're susceptible to having it come back. Three years ago, it did."

"The same kind?"

"No, this time it was different. I'll let CiCi explain. That is if you want me to set up this meeting."

He could see her considering the idea.

"Are you sure it wouldn't upset them to talk about their past?"

"I know these women. They are just like you. They would want to help."

"What do you mean, just like me?"

"They have big generous hearts."

13

"How's Jase doing?" Brax asked the men leaning around Gideon's granite kitchen countertop. He knew that his teammate was currently with his parents in Missouri, with Bonnie and the twins, but he hadn't heard much more than that.

Everybody looked over at their lieutenant who shrugged. Brax definitely wasn't going to get any answers from that quarter.

"I talked to him four days ago," Nolan said. "He sounded in great spirits, and I didn't believe a word of what he was saying. In Germany they did a great job on repairing the break. He has a lot of hardware in his body now. The doctors were really hopeful that he could get back to eighty to ninety percent of where he was. But it's the surrounding muscle that's the problem. In another week he's going to go to Walter Reed for some intensive physical therapy. He's bound and determined to get back to where he was."

Nolan took a long swallow of his beer. So did

Kostya. It was clear that neither one of them wanted to say that a full recovery wasn't likely.

Dammit.

It was time to change the subject, and Gideon did.

"She's got one hell of a case," Gideon said, referring to Jenny.

They all looked to the women huddled in the living room.

Brax had worried when so many women had shown up, but as he looked them over, he realized that they would be gentle with Jenny.

"I don't think she wants to sue New Era Cyber Tech," Brax said as he leaned his forearms against Gideon's counter. "She's just trying to get through each day. I'm hoping talking to the ladies will be the impetus she needs to go to a psychologist so that she can start living her life again."

"Is she still in the hotel?" Linc asked. "Or has she returned to her apartment?"

"That's the problem, she doesn't have an apartment to return to. She moved out when she took the long-term assignment in Dhaka. She hasn't left the hotel since she got there, except for the three times with me. This field trip makes four. The only apartment-hunting she's done has been online."

"Agoraphobia?" Nolan asked.

"Maybe," Brax admitted. "I'm really not sure. That's why I think she needs to talk to a professional. I've seen her have two panic attacks. One at a crowded mall and another when we went to a quiet restaurant. Then there's the fact that she doesn't feel safe in the hotel room. She shoves a heavy chair in front of the door each night."

"Maggie ended up with night terrors after Kyle tried to kidnap her. She'd wake up screaming. No matter what I'd do or say, they weren't getting better. She ended up seeing someone in Jasper Creek. The woman really helped Maggie," Nolan explained.

"I really thought you would stay there," Kostya said.

"Maggie likes it here. All the Omega Sky women have been great, but she misses the small-town feel of Jasper Creek. I'm not sure, but I think she would be happier down in Tennessee. If that's true, then we're moving. Trust me, boss, if that ever comes to pass, you'll be the first to know," Nolan told his lieutenant.

"Dammit, don't tell me that my old boss is trying to recruit you for his shitty security company. You're a SEAL, dammit," Kostya growled.

Brax, Linc, Gideon and Nolan laughed.

"I dare you to call Onyx Security a shitty security company in front of Simon Clark." Gideon grinned.

Kostya rubbed the back of his neck, then took a sip of his beer. "I'm not taking that dare." Then Kostya turned to look at Nolan. "Is he recruiting you?"

Nolan lifted up his hands, palms out. "He knows that Maggie has a lot of friends in Jasper Creek, so he told me that if we ever moved back to Tennessee, there would be a job waiting for me. Apparently, he's getting more business than he can handle."

"Good for him," Kostya smiled sincerely. "Good for him." Then he scowled. "But if he lures you away, he and I *will* be having words."

It took Jenny a while to figure out all the players when she sat down in Gideon and Jada's living room. Of course, since it was Jada's house, she caught onto who Jada was. She was the gorgeous black woman who had set out all of the munchies and shooed the men away.

Then there was Lark Barona. She was married to Kostya Barona. Jenny didn't really remember him from her rescue. Brax had explained that Kostya was his team leader, and that Lark was an investigative journalist. She wondered if she still did that line of work since she was so late in her pregnancy.

"You were kept in a hole in the ground?" Maggie clarified.

Leila nodded. "Not one of my favorite adventures." She shrugged.

"Don't downplay it," Lark Barona said quietly. "What happened to you was horrific."

Leila closed her eyes and shrugged. "I'm still working on that. Humor is how I cope. But when it happens to someone else, it's horrific." She turned away from Lark and leaned across the coffee table to Jenny. "Honey, I was in that hole for a day and a half. How long were you kept captive in Bangladesh?"

Jenny swung her head around, taking her time to look into the faces of each of the five women who had gathered today to give her support. All she saw was kindness and empathy.

"Three weeks. I was kept in a shack. To begin with, it had a clay floor, but it was monsoon season, so eventually it was a floor that was six inches of mud. I had a bucket for a toilet and they fed me roti bread, rice, and when I was lucky, lentil soup. I was so sick that in the end I thought I was just going to drown in the mud, and that didn't sound too bad, you know?"

She hated the fact that she'd been this close to giving up. Her tears welled up.

Brax's sister CiCi was sitting beside her. She grabbed her hand and held it tight, just like her brother would have.

"The important thing is that you didn't. You survived," CiCi murmured.

"What is it with being rained on?" Leila asked. "I swear, these assholes like it when we get rained on."

"What happened to your captors?" Jenny asked Leila.

"Dead. Every single one of them. What about yours?"

"I'm not sure."

Leila looked over at the men drinking beer in the kitchen. "Linc?"

He must have been listening in because he gave her some kind of sign. She turned back to Jenny. "Your captors are dead, too."

Jenny looked at her, stunned.

"But I think there were a lot of them," Jenny protested.

Jada picked up her half-full glass of wine and sat back in her chair. "Honey, that's how they roll. Someone goes after us, or some woman in distress, they take care of the problem. We're not privy to the particulars, but we know that in the end, we're safe."

"That's not true, sometimes we see what happens," Maggie piped up. "I had nightmares for a long time."

Lark leaned forward. "Because of how Nolan took care of that crazy man who tried to kidnap you?"

"No. Thinking of that calms me down. But thinking about how Kyle could have ended up taking me and I would have disappeared and never seen Nolan or Iris ever again."

"How did you stop the nightmares?" Jenny asked.

"I started with a counselor down in Jasper Creek. That's where we were when Nolan took leave for a while. Then when we moved here to Virginia and got married, Nolan found a way for me to choose from a couple of different psychologists. I found a man this time, and I see him from time to time. Not often, maybe every other month."

"That's what Brax thinks I need to do."

"Why?" Lark asked.

You could really tell she was the leader of the pack of women, just like her husband was the leader of the men.

"I've had a couple of panic attacks in front of Brax and he's concerned."

CiCi gave her hand a squeeze. "I'm betting if you've had a couple of panic attacks in front of Brax you've had a lot more when you weren't in front of him, right?"

"Yeah," she admitted quietly. "But it doesn't make sense. I'm out of Bangladesh. I'm here in the States. I should be fine."

"That's not how these things work," CiCi countered. "I had someone help me. I didn't have them for panic attacks, but after spending so much time in the hospital and thinking I was going to die, it took me a long time to accept that having a future was my new normal. I couldn't cope. Our brains and emotions sometimes need to be healed by a doctor just like our bodies do."

"Hmmm, I never thought about it like that," Jenny admitted.

"Yeah, I'm smart." CiCi smirked. "Just don't expect it to run in the family." CiCi raised her voice for the last two sentences.

Everybody in Gideon and Jada's house laughed, except for Brax, who glowered at his sister.

What would it be like to have a relationship with someone where I could tease them like that? Oh hell, be honest. I want to have a relationship with Brax where I could tease him like that.

"How come I get the feeling they're talking about me?" Brax asked the men in general.

"Because they are." Nolan grinned.

"Do all the rest of you think so, too?" Brax asked as he looked each one in the eye.

"Definitely." Linc laughed.

"No question." Gideon grinned.

Kostya just nodded.

"Great," Brax sighed. "That's just what I need."

"Sorry, Brax. That's just the way it goes during the

courtship time. Don't you remember how bad it was for Gideon?" Kostya asked.

Brax thought back to Jada's antics and grinned. "Yeah. Thank God, there is no way that Jenny will ever be as bad as that."

"You better be knocking on wood." Gideon smiled. "You just tempted the Gods of Love."

"How bad is it for her?" Nolan asked. Brax wasn't surprised at his question. Everybody knew the struggle that Maggie had. Nolan had been a mess worrying about his woman and being the primary caretaker for their young daughter as Maggie got back on her feet.

"I'm not really sure. The rest of you were in more of a relationship with your women. I'm not even in the courtship stage. We're just friends. I'm not even convinced that I want to be in the courtship phase."

"So basically, you're lying to yourself," Linc said. "Maybe you're the one who needs to see a shrink."

"Look, I'll admit we bonded a little when we were in Bangladesh, but now that we're in the States, it's different. Friends. We're just friends."

"How many times have you called her since we've been home? How many times have you gone out with her?"

"Not many."

"How many?" Gideon drawled. "Take a guess."

"I dunno." Brax thumbed his fingernail across the label of his empty beer bottle.

"We've been back for nineteen days. I say you've called her nineteen times and you've taken your *friend* out of the hotel four times. Anybody else want to put a wager on this?" Nolan asked as he looked around the kitchen,

"I think he's called more than once a day. My bet is thirty-eight calls and he's taken her out twice," Kostya guessed.

"I want in on the action," Gideon chuckled. "I say—"

"Enough already," Brax interrupted. I've only been able to talk her out of the hotel three times, and I've called her twice a day since we've been home. There. Are you satisfied?"

"Damn, that was going to be my bet," Linc said as he opened the fridge and brought out more beers.

"One is enough," Nolan said as he waved his hand. "I'm on toddler duty tonight. Mrs. Fuentes is a dependable babysitter, but she always gets Iris to sleep during the day, so by the time we get home, our little angel is raring to go."

"Thanks for the info," Kostya said. "I don't think Lark and I will be using her then. The last thing we need is having a kid who doesn't sleep at night."

"Good luck with that. I might have missed the time when Iris was a newborn, but I've been living through teething. It's hell, man." And with that bit of warning, Nolan went to the fridge and pulled out a bottle of water and took a healthy swig.

"I don't want to think about it. I say we bring our focus back onto Brax. So, what have you and Jenny been talking about?" Kostya wanted to know.

Brax turned back to the women and saw that Jada, Maggie, and CiCi were coming their way. *It must be meal prep time.* He definitely knew that Jenny and Lark didn't cook, so that's why they were still in the living room. He looked over at Linc and raised his eyebrow.

"Cooking isn't Leila's thing. Which is great, since I like doing it."

"That's great, then I'm putting you to work," Jada said as she rounded the kitchen island and smiled up at Linc. "Any of the rest of you want to volunteer?"

"What are you making?" Gideon asked.

"Street tacos and all the fixings."

"I'll leave you to it." Gideon gave his woman a lingering kiss.

"Enough making out, there are vegetables that need slicing," Linc objected. "Out."

14

"Thank you so much for today. I had the best time."

"I'm glad, Honey," Brax said as he pulled up to the hotel parking gate.

"You don't have to park, you can just drop me off up front."

"That's not the way this works. I pick you up at your door, I drop you off at your door."

He could feel her looking at him as he grabbed the ticket.

"It's a waste of money. I'm perfectly safe here."

There she was, always thinking about everybody else. This was all about saving him money, when he knew damn good and well, even walking up to her room by herself was going to scare her.

"Humor me, Jenny. It's part of being a big brother. I can't help myself."

"Oh. Yeah. That makes sense."

I'm going to have to remember that. I get my way when I use the big brother argument. Cool.

"Me opening your door is also part of the big brother service, so wait for me, huh?"

"Now you're just yanking my chain." She rolled her eyes.

"I'm not. They've salted the parking lot because of the ice. It's slippery, so please wait for me. Please." He saw her give in on the 'please.' He took his time walking around the truck. All evening he couldn't get his friends' voices out of his head. Yeah, he liked Jenny. He liked her a lot. He worried about her. But was she really someone he wanted to get involved with?

He opened the passenger door.

She looked down at him. "Okay, Hotshot, I waited. What's my prize?" Her smile could melt ice.

With that one smile, he wanted to kick his own ass. Who was he kidding, they already were involved. But he realized he wanted more. Now he needed to find out if there was any chance that Jenny might be on the same page.

"Your prize is that instead of stepping down on the running board, I'm going to lift you out of the truck and set you down nice and easy, so you won't slip."

She held out her arms and rested them on his shoulders so that he could clasp her waist and set her down on the pavement. He was as gentle and careful as he could be, keeping her broken ribs in mind.

Jenny stood there in his arms, looking up at him. "How was that a prize?"

"Well, maybe the prize could be for both of us, depending on your point of view."

"Now you're not making any sense, Braxton Walker.

What are you talking about?" She tugged at the collar of his leather jacket, so that it closed more tightly around his throat. He knew she did it so she didn't have to meet his eyes. It gave him hope. She wasn't insisting they walk to the hotel lobby immediately.

"Jenny, I was seeing it like this. I think since you let me help you, you deserve a kiss. I think because I helped you, I deserve a kiss."

She looked back up at him, her eyes twinkling as bright as the stars above. "You do, huh? I didn't know you were such a thinker."

"I am."

"That's a shame. Here I was hoping you were more of a doer."

Brax threw back his head and laughed. How could he have ever thought that he didn't want to have a relationship with this woman?

JENNY STARED up at Brax as he laughed, and she melted. Not only was he easy to talk to, but he laughed at her jokes. She had no idea how much longer he would be around babysitting her, so she'd do her best not to overthink things. She knew better than to trust her future in anybody's hands but her own. Instead, she would bask in his attention and make sure that she didn't come to expect it.

She blinked. He was looking down at her, his gaze intent.

He must have said something, but she hadn't heard

him. Both of his large, calloused hands cupped her cheeks.

"I'll show you a doer," he whispered. Then his lips settled onto hers. Lightly at first. His lips were soft, but the pressure was firm. Far too quickly, he pulled away.

"No," she whispered. "Come back." She'd dared him into this, and she wasn't going to let him stop at just one, barely there kiss.

She wrapped both arms around his neck and his eyes lit up with satisfaction. He lifted a hand and slid his fingers through her hair, and how good did that feel? She closed her eyes at the decadent sensation, then re-opened them, not wanting to miss anything. He was smiling when his lips came down and kissed her again.

Soft and sweet, like warm caramel, his lips coaxed hers to open, and she sighed.

And again.

Bold and sharp like spiced rum, his tongue delved deep, and she moaned.

And again.

Dark and decadent, like coffee-flavored truffles, and she dug her fingers into his scalp.

Brax stepped back.

"Why'd you stop?" Jenny wanted to know.

"You were whimpering."

"It was a good whimper. Don't stop."

Dammit, I'm sounding too needy.

"Honey, it's cold, let's get you inside."

"I'm not cold. In fact, I'm really warm."

Quiet. Be quiet. Be quiet. Don't sound desperate.

"Baby, it is cold. You just got out of the hospital. Now come with me."

He pulled her close. And wasn't that just the nicest thing? Brax kept his steps short so that she could keep up as they walked through the lobby. It was just one of the many, many considerate things he did for her. Before she knew it she was getting out her hotel key to open her room.

When she opened the door, she stopped short and grabbed Brax's forearm. She'd left all the lights on before leaving, but now she could only see the glow of the bedroom light.

"Honey? What is it?"

"The lights are off. They were on when I left."

"Wait in the hall, and I'll look through your suite, okay?"

"Okay." Jenny couldn't stop the shivers racing through her body.

"You're going to have to let go of me," he whispered.

She looked up into his brown eyes. "I can't, Brax."

"Sure you can, sweetheart. You're brave, remember?"

She shook her head hard enough that strands of brown-blonde hair whipped across her face. "No, I'm not."

"Okay, come with me. But stand behind me, okay?" He pulled her hand off his forearm and gripped her hand. She nodded.

Jenny gasped as she watched him pull out a gun. Where had he been hiding that?

She kept a tight grasp on his hand and followed

close behind him as he walked toward the open bedroom door.

He turned to her and put his mouth down to her ear. In a voice that she could barely hear, he said, "I need to find out if there is anyone behind the door. Let go for a moment."

She nodded and released his hand.

Jenny watched as Brax pulled the door almost all the way closed, then slammed it open into the wall. Nothing. He was across the room and into the bathroom before she could even blink.

Then he walked back out. "It's clear."

That's when Jenny noticed that her bed had been turned down and there was a piece of chocolate wrapped in gold foil lying on her pillow. She felt herself begin to tremble as she pointed at it.

"I'm so sorry." She felt like she was going to cry. "I made a mountain out of a molehill."

He walked over to her and wrapped one arm around her waist and the other around her head, tucking her close to his chest. "You have nothing to be sorry for. Jenny, being on a knife's edge is understandable."

"But I'm sick of it. I'm sick of who I am."

"I'm not."

"How can you not be? You've been babysitting me ever since you got back to the States, and you don't even know me..." She let her voice trail off.

"What?"

"Never mind."

"No, tell me, baby. I want to know."

"Nobody knows me. It's what I realized in that goddamned shack. I've never let anybody know me."

Brax didn't say anything. Instead, he stroked his hand from the top of her head down the line of her back.

Up and down.

Up and down. It felt so good, she was sure her bones were going to melt and she would dissolve into him.

When her trembling stopped, he lifted her chin with one finger. "I know you, Jenny Rivers."

"No, you don't."

"I do, baby. I do. I know that you like skiing in Colorado when the first snow falls. I know that wherever you're living in the States you like to go volunteer at a women's shelter. I know you still feel guilty for blowing Jarrod off, even though he got to sleep with you—and trust me honey, he got the long end of *that* stick. I know that you're a chocolate snob and you probably won't eat that piece of candy on your pillow because it's not See's Candy."

He was right. He knew her. This man *knew* her.

Jenny felt her throat close and her nose clog. She tried to keep herself under control, but she couldn't. When the first tear fell, it was like her entire body fell. It took her a moment to realize she hadn't fallen, but Brax had sat down on the side of the bed, and now he cradled her in his arms as she soaked in his warmth and caring.

Jenny had no idea how long she stayed like that. At no point did Brax tell her not to cry. Instead, he said nonsense words of comfort as he gently rocked her, stroked her, and brushed her tears away.

She had no idea how long they stayed that way. When she was finally aware of her surroundings, it was like she came out of a deep sleep to find her arms around his neck and her lips against his jaw.

"Kiss me?" It was a plea.

He kissed her temple.

She tilted her head back to look into his dark brown eyes. "No, a real kiss."

He gave her a slow smile. "Oh, there are real kisses in our future. You can count on that. But right now, I'm tucking you into bed."

Jenny shivered.

"And I'm staying the night," he finished.

Her eyes lit up.

"On the couch in the other room."

"You'll be more comfortable in the bed. Beside me." She coaxed.

"If I'm sleeping next to you, and not doing the many things I want to do, I won't be comfortable, I'll be in agony." He grinned down at her. "I'm sleeping on the couch. Now go get ready for bed. Just think of it; now you'll have a chair, a gun, *and* a SEAL protecting you."

"I'd feel safer if the SEAL was in bed with me."

"Give it up." Brax smiled. He stood up and sent her hopes back down to the ground. "Your feminine wiles won't work on me. Now get ready for bed and under the covers, and I'll come give you a kiss good night."

She sighed. "If you sleep beside me, I'll give you the chocolate," she wheedled.

"You'll give me the chocolate anyway."

"Yeah, that's true."

She watched as he sauntered out of the room and shut the door behind him. She sighed.

Maybe it's time for me to learn how to keep somebody in my life.

15

THE NEXT MORNING, BRAX KNOCKED ON JENNY'S bedroom door but she didn't answer, even after a couple of loud knocks, which surprised him. When peeked in, he saw her dead to the world. He wouldn't have thought that was possible, considering how tightly wound she'd been the night before. Then he thought about it. Jenny had mentioned that she hadn't been sleeping well. Maybe knowing that a gun, a chair, and a SEAL stood between her and the bad guys *had* provided her the peace of mind to get a good night's sleep.

"Wake-up sleepyhead. I'm hungry," he called from the doorway. She still didn't move, and he grinned. He stepped closer and called out again. Still nothing.

"Oh, Jenny," he said in a sing-song voice. "It's wakey, wakey time."

"Go 'way," she murmured and pulled a pillow over her head.

Brax knew how irritating the song was. CiCi had

sung it to him often enough when he was a teenager and wanted to sleep in on the weekend. So, he sang the words again. "It's wakey, wakey time. There are places to go and people to see."

"Go. Away." She enunciated clearly.

Yep, she was awake now.

"It's wakey—"

Brax easily caught the pillow that she flung at him and started laughing. "You've slept long enough. You haven't eaten since we left Gideon's place, you have to be hungry."

Jenny rolled over, and Brax caught a look of her tousled hair and sleep-soft face. She looked beautiful.

"Don't lie to me, I saw how much you ate last night. You must have a hollow leg that needs to be filled on an hourly basis. You're the one who's really hungry, admit it," she grumbled.

"You're right, I am. And I want company. So, get your cute ass out of bed and come with me."

She'd been ready to object. He'd watched her mouth open, but as soon as he called her ass cute, her eyes got wide, and she'd closed and opened her mouth like a guppy. Good to know, complimenting her ass was a way to stop an argument.

"Brax, don't you have something else to do today?"

"Nope, it's Sunday. Like every other normal person, I have the day off. I'll wait in the other room while you get ready to go."

"You do know I'm going to take a shower, right? This is going to take a while."

"You do know that I'm going to appreciate your efforts, right?" Brax said with a grin.

"You're such a man."

"I'm glad you noticed."

He sat back on the couch and rested his bare feet on the coffee table, hoping that the cleaning staff knew enough to clean all the surfaces between guests. He had turned his phone onto its battery saver setting the night before, so he turned it back to full steam while he waited for Jenny. He had a long message from CiCi telling him how much she liked Jenny and how great it would be if he could bring her over for dinner some night. Then there were three messages from Mateo. Each one pushier than the last. He wanted the scoop on his relationship with Jenny. It hadn't taken long for the Omega Sky rumor mill to kick in. He'd bet his bottom dollar it was Gideon who'd spilled the beans.

Before he could decide who to call back, his phone rang. It was Mateo.

"Yo," he answered.

"What's going on between you and Jenny?"

"Nothing."

"Yeah, I believe that. Try again."

"Seriously, there's nothing going on."

"Why didn't you pick up Faith last night?"

Brax thought about stringing Mateo on a little bit more. It was fun. But he would really like to talk things out with somebody.

"I spent the night at her hotel room... On the couch."

"Smartass. Try that on somebody else. I know you've been calling her. A lot. And you took her out at least once. So how deep are you in?"

"That's the thing, I don't know. Yeah, I admit it, I think I might be getting in deep. I tried to talk her into talking to a psychologist, but that was a no go. That's what yesterday with the women was all about. I'm hoping one of them might have convinced her it was okay to see a professional."

"Gideon told me who all was there. I think talking to them probably helped a lot," Mateo said.

"I've seen her have two panic attacks. It's going to take more than an evening with the ladies to get over her trauma. I think we might have something here, but I don't think she's in the headspace to be ready for anything serious."

Mateo didn't respond.

"What?"

"I didn't say anything," Mateo responded.

"I noticed. That means you have a lot to say, so say it."

"Seems to me that anybody, man or woman, who survived that hellhole, is pretty damn strong and is capable of making their own decisions about things. I know that Lainey would kick me in the balls if I tried to take a decision like that out of her hands."

"So, what? You say I should just be coming onto her like some Neanderthal?"

"I know you, Brax. You don't have a caveman bone

in your body. I'm just saying that while you're spending time with the woman, don't put up roadblocks where they're not needed."

Brax let out a deep breath. "Are you sure?"

"I'm positive. You'll be able to read the signs."

"Right now, she needs a friend." *And maybe some hugs and kisses.*

"Then be her friend. Bring her over when you pick up Faith. If she's not a dog person, then this whole conversation is moot."

"This is true," Brax agreed.

I really hope Jenny likes dogs.

He heard the shower turn off. "I've got to go."

"Are the two of you coming over?" Mateo asked.

"Yes."

"When? Lainey will want to cook something."

"How about a late lunch. Say three o'clock?"

"Perfect."

"I REALLY DON'T REMEMBER someone named Mateo," Jenny said for the third time. "Can you describe him?"

"Big guy, dark skin. He emigrated from Argentina when he was five."

"All of you were big guys. And it was dark, so all of you looked dark."

"Honey, don't worry about it. It's no big deal."

"It's rude."

Brax threw back his head and laughed and Jenny scowled at him. He'd been laughing almost non-stop since he'd told her they were going to visit his friend and his fiancée.

"Quit laughing at me."

"I'm laughing *with* you," Brax said as he looked over at her when they pulled up to a stop sign.

"I'm not laughing, therefore, you're laughing at me."

"Jenny, you're cute as a button. Please don't worry. You liked last night, didn't you?"

"Yeah," she eventually admitted. "But you said that Mateo was one of your best friends."

"I did. That's why I know he's going to love you."

"Yeah, the woman with the panic attacks that you've been babysitting. The one who made you sleep on a tiny couch."

"I slept on the floor. The couch was too small."

"That's even worse," she wailed.

"Are you kidding? Sleeping on soft carpet in a warm room is heaven compared to where I've slept in the past." Brax held out his hand and she looked at it. "Take it."

She stared at it.

"Be brave, Jenny, hold my hand. We've kissed. You can surely hold my hand."

She bit the inside of her cheek, then took his hand, and he threaded their fingers together. They continued along, and she stared at his profile. He was so handsome. She could gaze at him forever.

He glanced over at her. "Do I have something on my cheek?"

She could feel herself blushing, but dammit, she

wasn't going to be all blushing-high-school-girl. "I like how you look."

"That's a relief, since you know I almost had a heart attack when you came out of the bedroom in that outfit this morning. It sure as hell was worth the wait." He squeezed her hand a little tighter. It shot tingles throughout her body.

"I bought some clothes online."

"You did good. Let me say again, the boots are stellar."

Jenny had to force down a grin. She'd had Brax in mind when she'd bought the tight, black, knee-high leather boots with the crisscross laces up the sides. They went perfectly with her skinny jeans and red sweater. She'd even blown-out her hair so it had extra body. Only lip gloss though, since they had just been going to breakfast.

Hopefully her outfit would be okay when she met Lainey. She'd bought the boots to impress a man, but maybe Lainey wouldn't like them. Would she think they were too over the top? Too slutty?

"Whatever you're thinking, stop."

"I'm not thinking anything. I'm sitting here wondering when we're going to get to Mateo and Lainey's house."

"Liar. You're getting yourself worked up again."

She blew out a breath. "You're not supposed to know me so well. It's against the rules."

"You know me just as well. We've been talking on the phone twice a day for almost a month. Some of our conversations have lasted over an hour. I think that's close to twenty dates, don't you?"

"I think you've been sniffing cleaning fluid, or licking lizards. What makes you think I would have gone out on twenty dates with you?"

"'Cause you like me." His fingers tightened around hers, and he brought her hand up to his face and he whispered a kiss across her knuckles. "Mateo and Lainey are going to love you."

"I hope so," she said with a sly smile. "But this is a make or break it moment."

"You'll get along with them just fine, stop worrying."

"I'm not worrying about them, I'm worried about your dog. 'Cause don't lie to me Braxton Walker; you're sweating bullets over there hoping that I'll get along with your dog."

He turned his head and gave her a sharp look. "You don't know that."

"Yes, I do. You're totally one of those, 'love me, love my dog' types. You've talked about Faith a lot. It's one of the things that made you so approachable. I don't think I would have glommed onto you so much if I hadn't heard how much you love her."

He gave her hand another squeeze. "Well, then I'm happy."

MATEO AND BRAX stood at the grill as they watched Lainey and Jenny playing fetch with the three dogs.

"You're going to overcook the burgers," Brax said for the second time.

"I'm from Argentina, grilling meat is in my bones. The burgers will come out perfectly," Mateo assured him. "Go play with the dogs."

"I like watching."

"You're just happy that your woman and dog are bonding."

Brax grinned. "You're not wrong."

Jenny was good with all three of the dogs, including Xena, who was often skittish around new people. But Jenny didn't have the 'mom' voice, so the dogs didn't obey her when she told them to get down. Her jeans and sweater were covered with dog hair. But she didn't seem to mind.

"It's hard to believe she's the same person we rescued seven weeks ago," Mateo said as he pointed his spatula at the cheese.

Brax handed him a couple of slices.

"Yesterday helped her a little," Brax admitted. "Knowing she's someplace safe makes all the difference."

"Yeah, it did for Lainey, too. But you're her touchstone."

Brax watched as Mateo turned the patties and put the cheese on two of them.

"Ya think?"

"I know. You two bonded back in Bangladesh, and with all the calls, I'd say it's even more since you've both been in the States."

"Maybe."

"How long are each of your calls?" Mateo asked.

"I told her in the truck on the way over, that the calls were the equivalent of twenty dates."

"You're shitting me," Mateo said as he looked over at him.

"Okay, maybe only fifteen," Brax admitted.

"Nah, probably twenty," Mateo disagreed. "You even knew that she doesn't like cheese on her burgers, I didn't have to ask."

"She's allergic to dairy."

"I rest my case," Mateo smirked. "Lunch is ready," he hollered out.

Brax laughed when the first ones to the deck were the three dogs. "You do not get people food," Mateo admonished. "There is food in your bowls." He pointed to the three bowls that were on the deck.

"Isn't it kind of cold to be grilling?" Jenny asked as Mateo brought the burgers and grilled onions into the house.

"As far as Mateo is concerned it could be snowing and it's still a good time to be grilling," Lainey laughed as she brought out a macaroni salad from the refrigerator. She set it down on the set table, then went back to the kitchen and pulled something that smelled wonderful from the oven. She slid the slices into a bowl.

"What's that?" Jenny asked as she brought it to the table.

"Provenzal-style Papas, they're Argentinian spiced potatoes," Lainey answered.

"You'll love them," Mateo assured her.

"If they taste as good as they smell, I'm sold," Brax said.

"Are you sure there isn't anything I can help you with?" Jenny asked Lainey.

"I'm sure, just sit down and enjoy."

Soon they were all seated around the table, and Mateo and Brax were explaining about Gideon's dog Lucy and how well trained she was. They didn't go into the story on how she had sniffed out bombs that had saved a bunch of adults and children from being blown up when Gideon's house had been sabotaged.

"I didn't realize she was so well trained when I met her yesterday," Jenny admitted. "She seemed so friendly and playful."

"That's part of her training as well," Mateo said. "Our hope is to train Hercules and Faith as well as Gideon trained Lucy."

"First, you're going to have get them to obey you when you say 'heel' and 'sit.'" Lainey laughed.

Mateo leaned over and pulled Lainey in for a kiss. "I'll show you how well I obey tonight," he said after he was done.

Brax saw Jenny blush. It was cute. Hell, it was a mild kiss, not like the one he and Jenny had shared. And not like the one he intended to share with Jenny tonight.

Lainey shook her head. "Don't mind him, he's going through his teenage years, just like the dogs."

"And you love it," Mateo murmured.

"If you don't behave, you won't get any of the chocotorta that I baked."

Brax watched in fascination as his friend's eyes went

wide. "How did I not notice that you baked that? Where was I?"

"I baked it yesterday, while you were watching the soccer game with your friends."

"I promise to be good." He turned to Brax and Jenny. "You are in for a treat. Lainey is a Goddess in the kitchen. You will think you have died and gone to heaven when you taste her chocotorta."

Brax laughed as his friend's accent became more pronounced. Yep, Mateo had definitely found the right woman for him.

16

I can do this.

I can do this.

I can really do this.

Jenny pushed open the heavy glass door of her hotel and pulled her scarf tighter. It was only four blocks to the coffee shop to meet Jada. She could do this. The last three days when she'd gone to get coffee, CiCi and Lark had met her at the hotel and walked with her. This was the first time she was walking alone. But she could do it. She wasn't a little baby.

Oh, for God's sake, enough with the bullshit talk. Of course I'm not a baby. I've lived all over the world. I've managed teams of twenty or more people. I'm competent. I can walk four blocks!

She went out into the crush of bodies and turned left to start walking. She realized she was going too slow as everybody passed her, and she got jostled. She needed to speed up, if she didn't want to be pushed around. There we go, now she was actually passing people. Not bad. The wind hit her sideways and her hair got in her eyes. She brushed it out of the way.

Wham.

"Look where you're going," the big bald man said after he practically mowed her down.

Jenny gripped her purse tighter to her body, not caring that her ribs now hurt. She was just glad she hadn't fallen.

She choked back an automatic 'I'm sorry'. Because she wasn't. It was his fault. Anyway, 'I'm sorry' was no longer in her vocabulary.

I'm a survivor. Fuck the assholes.

She looked up and realized she was at the first crosswalk. After that, just two more blocks and she'd be at Coffee Time. She hoped that Jada was already there and had grabbed a table. Jenny started to walk faster. The light must have turned since the crowd of people was shoving forward. She could hardly breathe with all the bodies pushed together and the scent of wet wool coats. She blindly followed along. As soon as she got to the other side, she shuffled toward the nearest building that had an empty entryway and took a moment to breathe. She just needed a moment.

Okay, now she could handle it. She entered the group of pedestrians again and headed down to the next corner. She sped up. This time she was going to be at the front of the mass of people crossing the street. She was going to see what was going on, and not be in the middle of a herd. It took some doing, and she had to throw an elbow or three, but she made it to the front.

Jenny waited impatiently for the walk sign,

knowing that she would have to be careful of the idiots taking right hand turns at the last moment. But she saw Coffee Time on the corner. She saw Jada in the coveted window seat and she waved, and Jada waved back. Boy did she need a hit of caffeine. Just how long was she going to have to wait at this light?

Her entire world shifted in slow motion as hands shoved her in the middle of her back. She didn't utter a sound as she slammed into the hood of a blue sedan taking a right-hand turn. Her body felt liquid as she slid back down onto the pavement. Her hip and shoulder smashed into the concrete first, then her head. Some unconscious need for survival had her arms covering her head and yanking her knees up to her chest, trying to make herself the smallest target possible. But even then, Jenny knew she was going to be run over.

All sound stopped and time stood still as she waited for her death. Nothing. Then she heard the shriek of brakes and the scream of people.

So many people talking.

Somebody touching her.

Moving her.

It hurt.

"Jenny, can you answer me?"

"Jada?"

"Just stay right here. An ambulance is on the way."

Coffee.

She'd been going to get coffee.

"WHAT THE FUCK HAPPENED?"

"You need to calm down."

Was that Brax? Why was he mad?

"Can you open your eyes?"

"Tell me what happened. How in the hell did she end up in the hospital? I thought you were taking her to coffee."

"Miss Rivers, I need you to open your eyes."

Oh, I'm supposed to open my eyes.

Jenny tried, but it felt like there were weights on her eyelids.

"Can't. Tired."

That didn't sound like her.

"Try again."

That sounded better. She tried again. She opened her eyes and saw a young woman bending over her. "Can you follow this light?"

Jenny watched the light.

"You've got a good-sized bump on your temple."

Jenny lifted her head.

"Whoa. Why don't you lie back."

"Why did you cut my clothes?"

"You were pretty banged up. We needed to see where you were hurt," the young woman said.

"Are you a doctor?"

"Yep. How are you feeling?"

"Everything hurts. What happened?"

"You were hit by a car."

"I was?" Jenny tried to remember being hit by a car, but all she remembered was waving to Jada.

"Yes. We're trying to determine the extent of your

injuries. We're going to send you up to radiology for some tests, and then we'll know more."

"I think I heard my friends out there. Can they come in?"

"No, they've been sent to the waiting room. They can come and see you when your tests are done and we have a room here in the ER for you."

Jenny's heart lurched. She didn't want to have to be in a hospital alone again. It had been horrible being separated from Brax when she first came to America.

"Are you sure that I'll see Brax after the tests?"

"Is he your boyfriend?"

Jenny nodded. Hoping that would mean more, so they would let him in sooner. Or maybe she was just saying that because it was something to make her feel better, to take away the pain.

"Now tell me what the fuck happened."

"I was waving to Jenny, and the next thing I saw was her lurching forward into this car. It made no sense. She wasn't walking into it like she wasn't paying attention to traffic or something. She was shoved."

Brax watched and listened as Jada recounted what had happened. There wasn't any way that he didn't believe what she was saying. He knew the woman. She lived for details. If Jada said that Jenny had been shoved, then Jenny had been shoved. But why in the hell would anyone want to shove Jenny into the oncoming traffic?

"I had to ask," Brax started.

"I know you don't want to believe it," Jada said. "I didn't want to, either. But there isn't a doubt in my mind that she was pushed. The problem is, it happened so fast, and there were too many people behind her, that I didn't see who did it."

They moved out of the way as a woman with a sobbing child tried to get past them. "Let's go outside," Brax suggested. The amount of coughing and sneezing people in the waiting room was getting on his nerves. He knew that they were good for at least a half hour before they would be called back to see Jenny.

As soon as they were outside, Jada started talking. "I called Gideon after I called you. He said he had to finish something up with Kostya, then he would be here."

Brax nodded. He appreciated the fresh air. He could finally breathe. Ever since Jada's call, he'd been out of his mind with worry. Even though Jada had said that Jenny wasn't badly injured, he had to see for himself.

"Can you think of any reason that someone would target Jenny? Or is this some rando?" Jada asked.

"The only people after Jenny have been reporters, but they wouldn't be pushing her, they would be stopping her to get a story."

"What about her old company? Gideon told me she had a case against them. Has she hired an attorney?"

Brax shook his head. Jenny didn't want to get into something like that. She was just beginning to recover from the kidnapping, let alone dealing with any kind of restitution from New Era Cyber Tech.

"Why not?" Jada asked. Brax could see the bloodlust in her eye, and he gave a weak laugh. "Seriously, Brax. Why not? Those assholes hung her out to dry. She should be all over that. I know I would be."

"You would be what?" Gideon said as he stepped up behind his fiancée.

"I would be suing the hell out of Jenny's company if they had known what a risk it was to stay in Bangladesh and then didn't pay the ransom. I would be milking them for all they were worth."

Gideon slid his arm around Jada and she leaned into him. "I know you would. I don't think Jenny is up for that quite yet." He looked over at Brax. "How's she doing?"

"They were sending her up to radiology when they kicked us out of the ER. Supposedly they'll let us know when she's been given a room in the ER."

"Not with that mess." Jada nodded toward the room inside. "We're going to have to be bothering the coordinators every five minutes for updates."

"Let's offer to buy them coffee and make it every ten minutes. How about that?" Gideon suggested.

"I like every five minutes," Brax said as he headed back into the waiting room.

"I'm her fiancé," he lied to the nurse. "She'll want me in her room."

"The doctor is waiting to get her admitted. Your

fiancée hit her head. We didn't see any significant brain swelling, but we want to keep her for twenty-four to forty-eight hours for observation. She also reinjured her ribs, so whatever gains she might have made when it comes to pain management, have been set back."

Fuck.

"She said she is staying at a hotel?" The doctor gave him a curious glance.

"She was," he nodded. "Now she's staying with me. I'll be able to take care of her. When I'm at work, my sister will be able to look in on her."

The doctor smiled. "That will be ideal. We still don't have a bed for her upstairs, so we can't admit her yet, but let me take you back to where we have her set up in the ER."

Brax nodded and followed the woman.

Shit. Shit. Shit.

He had no idea how Jenny was going to take his unilateral decision that she was going to move in with him. As he passed by the closed ER doors where other patients were, he realized he didn't give a damn. He should have demanded that Jenny stay at his house as soon as she was released from the hospital five-and-a-half weeks ago. He had no idea where things were headed between the two of them, but goddammit, it sure as hell wasn't just friends, that was for damn sure.

"Miss Rivers, we have a visitor. It's your fiancé."

Jenny looked up. For a split second she looked confused, then she saw Brax over her doctor's shoulder.

"Well, it's about time my fiancé showed up. I've been wondering where you were."

She was magnificent. She might have just been hit by a car. Still scared to go out alone. But her mind was a steel trap.

"They've been keeping me away while they've been checking you out, Darling."

"Darling, huh?"

The doctor laughed. "I'll leave you two alone. Someone will come and get you when there is a room available. I'm glad to hear that you're moving out of the hotel and in with your fiancé." She walked out of the little room and slid the door closed.

Brax stepped up to the head of the bed and put his knuckles underneath her chin so he could tip her head up and get a good look at her injury. He winced. "How are you feeling?"

"Like I got hit by a car."

"Stop it. I'm serious." He studied her green eyes, trying to gauge her level of pain. But like she had in Bangladesh, she was hiding it.

"I hurt. My head hurts, but my ribs feel like they're on fire. Same old, same old." Her husky laugh brushed across his nerves, soothing him after his panic. "So, you're my fiancé and I'm moving in with you. You move fast, Walker."

"I'm a SEAL, it's in the job description." She opened her mouth, but before she could say anything foolish like protest, he continued. "Jada is positive someone deliberately pushed you into the car. I don't like that. I don't like that at all. I want you with me, where I can watch over you. It's either you stay with me, or I sleep on the floor of your hotel. Are you really going to do that to me?"

She sucked in her lip and looked up at him with a pensive stare. "I don't want to put you out."

"You won't be. I promise."

"You told me that you like having your space. You admitted that on one of our first phone calls. You said that was one of the reasons you never had a long-term relationship."

"You're different. You don't get on my nerves. As a matter of fact, I like talking to you, and the few times that we've spent time together face-to-face, I've enjoyed the hell out of it. I relish the idea of having you in my space. But maybe you don't. You've been a loner all of your life. Maybe you don't want to stay at my place for a while."

"You make me feel safe. But can I be honest?"

He watched as she tried to sit up and winced.

"Hold on, let me lift the bed."

She winced some more as he lifted the head of the bed. "Do I need to call the doc for some pain meds?" he asked.

"That's the last thing I need right now. God knows what I would be saying."

"Are you saying that you would be even more honest?" he teased.

"Shut up and let me talk. All I was going to say is that you've come to mean a lot to me. I've been trying to work things through in my head. If it is because you were my rescuer, or if it is because you are who you are. Are you sure you want someone who has their feelings tangled up about you, hanging around?" The last part she asked in a husky whisper, and Brax felt the words down to his toes.

Fuck. How could he get so lucky? But she was right, he wanted to make sure that how she was feeling was truly about him, Brax, and not some guy who helped to rescue her. Was she seeing the difference between them?

"Say something," she pleaded.

"Then I think you living with me is the perfect thing for you to work things out. If you still feel like you care about me when you see me sitting on my couch for hours at a time in my underwear playing video games, then we'll know it's the real thing."

"Do you order in pizza with anchovies?" she asked hopefully.

"Anchovies, pineapple and tuna."

Jenny burst out laughing. She continued to laugh even when her hand went to her temple to massage against the pain. "If. If. If you're in boxer briefs I might look past the tuna, but if you're wearing tighty-whities, then all bets are off."

Brax threw back his head and laughed.

That was how an orderly found them when he opened the door to say they had a room upstairs for Jenny.

17

JENNY WAS RELEASED ON A WEDNESDAY AND BRAX TOOK the day off so he could take her to his house. He had already checked her out of the hotel and brought all her belongings to his house and set them up in his guest room.

When the nurse wheeled her out of the hospital, his truck was waiting out front, and he didn't allow her to hoist herself up into the passenger seat, instead he lifted her in. She'd forgotten how strong he was. When she turned to wave at the nurse, she winked at her as she waved back.

"Enjoy," Rebecca said. "Don't do anything I wouldn't do."

She and Brax were soon on the road, and as much as she tried to keep her eyes open, it was a lost cause.

"Am I going to have to sing the wakey, wakey song?"

Jenny sat straight up. "God no. I promise I'm awake."

She blinked her eyes a couple of times and realized

she was in the driveway of a one-story house painted light-green with navy trim. It had a path from the sidewalk to the front door hedged with pansies.

"You live here?"

Brax's lips twitched. "Nope, I always park in someone else's driveway when I come home."

"You are such a smartass."

"Why didn't you think I lived here?"

"The pansies."

Brax grinned. "They were on sale. Now stay there and I'll help you out of the truck."

Jenny thought about it and agreed. The idea of jumping down with her headache and her ribs aching did not appeal. Brax was soon opening her door, and she took in the scruff on his face. How had she missed that when he had picked her up? Hell, how had she missed the fact that he was wearing a tight, heather-gray Henley shirt under his leather jacket?

"Let's take it easy, okay?"

He gripped her hips and eased her down. Her breasts brushed against his chest on the way. She needed to make sure he took her lots of places in the next couple of days, so she could be lifted into and out of his truck.

"Are you steady, or do you need me to carry you inside?"

Carry me. Carry me. Her inner slut exclaimed.

What in the hell is wrong with me? I must have hit my head harder than I thought.

"I'm fine to walk."

Brax took small steps to match hers, then stood before the front door.

"Are you prepared?" he asked Jenny.

"For Faith? Absolutely."

"I told her that you're injured. She knows to be on her best behavior," Brax said as he opened the door.

Woof. Woof. Woof.

Brax stood in the entry. "Good girl. Now sit."

It was the most authoritative voice that Jenny had ever heard Brax use with his dog. When she peeked around his side, she saw that Faith was sitting.

"Welcome to my home."

As soon as Faith saw her, she started wagging her tail, but she remained seated.

"Aren't you a good girl," Jenny cooed. She went to bend down to pet her, and immediately regretted it. When were her ribs going to stop hurting?

"Let's get you on the couch with a heating pad, how does that sound?" Brax asked.

Jenny closed her eyes and sighed. "That sounds lovely."

She walked further into the house and blew out a breath that she hadn't realized she'd been holding. She slowly turned around and smiled with pleasure. She could tell it was still a work in progress. There were pictures propped against one wall, and the living room could use another chair or two, but the kitchen with its stainless-steel appliances had definitely been newly updated.

"Have you recently moved in?" she asked.

"Six months ago." Brax herded her toward the

couch. Jenny saw that there were two bed pillows already in place for her. "Why don't you lie down, and I'll get the heating pad." Faith followed them to the couch. Apparently the 'sit' command only lasted so long.

Jenny slowly arranged herself on the couch and nestled against the pillows. She felt a lot more comfortable than she had in the hospital. Hell, she felt more comfortable than she had in the hotel. Maybe it was because she was in Brax's house.

Before she knew it, he was shaking out a blanket that he had tucked at the end of the couch and laying it over her. "Since they were letting you out at lunchtime, I thought you might like some comfort food. I have beef stew in the crockpot, or I could warm up a chicken pot pie. What sounds good for lunch?"

"Are you kidding me? You have that for lunch?"

"Well, whatever you don't choose will be for dinner. Today I'm showing off with the chicken pot pie, but I would be lost without my crock pot."

"Are you saying you made the chicken pot pie?"

"I didn't make the crust. That was store bought, but the rest, yeah. That's easy enough."

"What happened to tuna on your pizza?"

Brax grinned. "One of the guys in Coronado likes tuna on his pizza. It was the grossest thing I'd ever heard of. I thought I might get a chuckle out of you. But you got me with the tighty-whities."

Jenny smirked, then snuggled down into the pillows.

"So have you decided?"

"Are you eating with me?" she asked.

"If you want."

"I want."

"In that case, I'll set up our dinner on this coffee table. So, which is it, stew or pies?"

"You decide."

He nodded. "I want stew for dinner. So, I'll warm up the pot pies. In the meantime, let me get you a heating pad." He walked over to the mantel, got the TV remote, and brought it over to her. "Help yourself."

"What about video games?"

"I play those over at Gideon's house. He has a whole entertainment room. Didn't Jada show you?"

"Yeah, you're a reader and like to hike. Whenever I'm back in fighting form, maybe we can hike together."

"I would love to take you on part of the Appalachian Trail. You'd love it."

"That would be great." Jenny yawned.

"Let me go grab lunch. I'll be back."

She watched him leave the living room, taking note of how he walked and how well his jeans accentuated his butt. She set the remote down beside her, and Faith came over and nuzzled her hand.

"Hi, Girl. How are you?"

The dog whined.

"I'm not up for playing today. I'm sorry."

Faith licked her hand, then batted her head against her palm.

"Oh, you want head scratches. That I can do." Jenny threaded her fingers through the silky black curls of Faith's coat until she was scratching her scalp, then

Faith plopped down in a heap beside the couch. This forced Jenny to reach farther down to keep up her petting. She knew she was doing a good job when Faith let out an appreciative moan.

"Are you seducing my dog?" Brax asked as he came in with a cuddly stuffed dog in his hand.

"What's that?"

"Believe it or not, it's a heating pad. CiCi got it for me at Christmas. It's called a Warmie®. I can put it in the microwave or the freezer." He pulled back her blanket. "Where do you need it?"

Jenny pointed to the most painful point on her ribs. He snuggled it close, and she felt instant relief. Faith raised her head and looked.

Woof.

"I'm not sure that she likes the competition," Jenny laughed. "How often have you used this?"

"Don't tell CiCi, but this is the first time that this has been used."

"I think she probably knows." Jenny smiled.

"The pot pies should be ready in about twenty minutes. Didn't you find anything you wanted to watch on TV?"

"I've watched enough TV to last me a lifetime. Do you have any books?"

"What kinds?"

Jenny laughed again. She realized she laughed a lot around Brax. "Give me an assortment. Anything will do. That is, if you have books in print."

"You're in luck. Dad gave me two boxes when he saw that the home office in this place had built-in shelves. He thought some of the shelves should have books. I hope you like Westerns."

"Louis L'Amour?"

"Yep, and Zane Grey. But he also has some military action and adventure, police thrillers. I'm pretty sure I saw a romance or two. But a whole hell of a lot of westerns."

"Bring the boxes."

Brax grinned.

JENNY DIDN'T EVEN MAKE it long enough for stew that night. Brax ended up carrying her to the guest bedroom. Earlier he had talked her into getting more comfortable, so she was wearing leggings and an oversized t-shirt, so when he put her to bed, at least she would sleep comfortably. It had been a nice afternoon. When she'd assured him that she could tune out him watching a documentary on TV while she read a book, she hadn't been kidding. She was a good quarter of the way through one of the Louis L'Amour books by the time she passed out.

He took the book into the guest room with her, in case she woke up during the night and wanted to continue reading. He really wanted to leave her bedroom door open so that he could hear her during the night in case she needed something, but he wasn't sure if she would be comfortable having Faith wander into her room at some point.

Faith had never slept on the bed in the guest room,

but he had let her sleep in his bed on more than one occasion, so he was afraid that she might get the idea to sleep with Jenny. With Jenny still being on edge, that was the last thing she needed, waking up in the middle of the night with an eighty-pound dog jumping up into bed with her. She'd be traumatized for sure.

After he got Jenny settled, he went back to the living room and got out his phone. He owed some people some calls and texts. First his sister. CiCi knew what had happened, and she'd been worried sick. She'd visited Jenny at the hospital both days she'd been a patient, and she wanted to be at his house when she arrived, but he'd nixed that idea.

"It's about time you called. She's not answering her cell phone. Can I talk to her?" CiCi asked before he had a chance to get a word in edgewise.

"The doctor suggested no tablet or phone time for the next couple of days. So, she turned them off. I fed her chicken pot pie, and she stayed awake until just now. I put her to bed, and now I'm calling you. See what a thoughtful big brother I am?"

"Can she not talk on her phone, or just not do things on her phone?"

"She needs rest right now. She can call you in a few days. She's still hurting."

"I feel like it's my fault. If I hadn't gone to the library, I would have been walking with her to the coffee shop, and this wouldn't have happened."

"Ceese, you're not to blame. If this was purposeful, they would have found some other time to get to her."

"You think someone did this on purpose?"

Brax winced. He hadn't wanted to tell his sister that; she was going to worry herself sick.

"Why would someone want to hurt Jenny? That doesn't make any sense."

"I said *if*. Trust me, we're looking into this."

"Are you going to keep her safe?"

"Damn right I will."

"Thank God. Okay. Tell her I said hello."

"I will. I love you, CiCi."

"I love you more."

He ended the call smiling. Now for a call that wouldn't leave him smiling, unless Gideon had found some answers.

"Hey, Brax. I'm surprised you didn't call sooner," Gideon said in lieu of 'hello'.

"Just put Jenny to bed. She finally took a pain pill, and I got some food in her. She's probably down for the night. Were you able to find out anything?"

"I know that New Era Cyber Tech has been frantically trying to track down Jenny so that they can have a discussion with her. Your friend Meyer has done a fantastic job of keeping her whereabouts confidential and stonewalling them."

"So, what does Cyber Tech want?" Brax asked.

"Their current VP of PR, guy named Roy Jeckel, has been trying to put out a wildfire with one fire extinguisher. Cyber Tech is bleeding money as their customers are leaving them. Turns out a lot of people aren't impressed with a company that will abandon their employee when they're kidnapped."

"I haven't been keeping up with every little bit of things, but isn't this going on a little long?" Brax asked.

"You'd think, but two things are making this a big story. One, this is a multi-billion-dollar company with over one hundred thousand employees worldwide. They've been acquiring companies left and right for the last ten years, so they're always big news. Second, is that one of the two high-ranking employees that they pulled out of Bangladesh two weeks before Jenny's kidnapping gave an interview to the Washington Post."

"He did?"

"Yeah. His name is Henry Roberts and he explained how he and Virginia Tyree had strongly suggested that the Bangladesh satellite office be shut down for a while because of the instability in the region. He went on to explain how the two of them were hustled back to Virginia two weeks later with promotions, leaving Jenny as the highest-ranking employee in the Bangladesh office. In other words, Henry felt that Jenny was left with a target on her back."

Brax whistled. "That guy either has quite a set of ethics, or an ax to grind."

"From what I've been able to gather, it's ethics. The guy's been a straight arrow all his life, even made Eagle Scout, and when his kids were little, he was always the coach of his daughter's soccer team. He's already left New Era Cyber Tech and went back to his old company at his old rate of pay. Basically, thumbing his nose at the promotion."

"I think I like this guy." Brax smiled. "When did the article come out?"

"Six days ago."

"Let's play this out. Which would make this problem worse for Cyber Tech?" Brax asked his brainy friend. "Jenny dying, or Jenny filing a lawsuit?"

"Jenny's death would have to look like an accident. I'd give it another two weeks to blow over. But if Jenny filed a lawsuit, I think they'd settle so fast it would make her head spin. She'd be a rich woman, and they'd have her sign an airtight NDA, and they could go public with a final statement to the press. I don't see how the company would want her dead."

"But, she hasn't sued, and it's been weeks," Brax pointed out.

"Therein lies the problem."

18

"Somebody tried to kill me!"

Jenny could not remember ever being so pissed off. Not even when her mother had died and left her alone in her childhood home with George Rivers. It hadn't been logical to be mad at her mother for dying, but as she ducked her father's slaps, fists, and kicks, she'd been beyond logic. Anger had just welled up. Kind of like today.

"Eat," Brax said as he pushed her plate of food toward her across the kitchen table.

"I'm too mad to eat."

"Fainting from hunger is not going to help you find out what is going on."

Jenny squinted and gave Brax an assessing look. "You know something, don't you?"

"If you eat your eggs, I'll tell you what I know."

"I'm not a child."

"No, you're not. Trust me, I in no way think of you as a child. I do, however, worry about you. So, for my piece of mind, would you please eat? You slept through dinner."

Jenny saw nothing but concern on his face and felt herself melt. The last person who had really cared about her like Brax did was her college roommate, Tina.

Damn, I need to call her.

"Okay, I'll eat, but you better fess up to everything when I'm done," Jenny said as she pulled her plate closer and picked up her fork.

"As long as you take your medicine as well."

"I don't need anything. I'm fine. I don't hurt."

Brax shook his head. "I can't believe that you can look me straight in the eye and lie to me like that. This does not bode well for our marriage."

The orange juice that she had just sipped went down the wrong tube and she started to cough...and cough. It took a long minute for her to recover. "Did you say marriage? Are you licking lizards again?"

"Nope, I just like to plan things out. Obviously, we were meant to be together, and the next step is marriage. Be happy I haven't gotten to the procreation stage."

She didn't know what to say, so she just stared at the madman sitting across from her.

"Your eggs are getting cold."

"How do you expect me to eat when you're spouting off nonsense like this?"

"I'm not spouting nonsense. I'm giving you something to think about besides someone shoving you into the street. Now eat up."

"You're crazy, you know that?"

"I defuse bombs for a living. I've been called crazy more than once in my life."

She already knew he was an explosive ordnance disposal technician, along with a couple of other skillsets that boggled her mind. Frankly, they scared her, and she tried not to think too much about them. Of course, those skills, and the skills of his other teammates had rescued her and kept her alive, so she really ought to be grateful, not scared.

Jenny sighed and started in on her eggs. "Hey, wait a minute. What did you do to make these eggs come out so nice and fluffy? Mine never come out like this?"

"Add a tiny bit of milk and flour. Works like a charm."

"Huh." Jenny continued to eat as she tried to work out why someone would want to hurt her. It made no sense. Finally, she was done and she moved to get up so she could carry her plate to the kitchen.

"Whoa, what are you doing?"

"I was going to rinse off my plate and put it into the dishwasher."

Brax shook his head. "No, you don't. Right now, you are the invalid and it's my job to baby you until you're back up to your fighting weight. Do you need to lie down?"

"You're kidding, right? I just spent ten solid hours in bed. I need to stand."

"Okay, but you're not going to do dishes. You can stand on the other side of the kitchen island and admire my domestic skills. That way if you get woozy you can lean on the counter. Got it?"

Jenny thought about it and realized she might actually have to lean.

Dammit.

"Okay." She got up slowly and followed Brax over to the kitchen island and watched as he rinsed plates and put them into the dishwasher. He had his shirtsleeves rolled up and she noticed the corded muscles of his forearms and his strong hands. Hands that she wouldn't mind having touch her body. All over her body.

Damn, I am getting woozy.

She leaned against the counter.

"See, I was right."

"I guess so," she agreed.

"Let's get you back on the couch. You don't have to lie down, you can just sit and veg out for a bit."

"Don't you need to go into work?"

"I took the day off."

"Brax, just how many days off can you possibly take?"

"I had a lot of PTO accrued. I'm covered. And then when I'm not, CiCi will be stopping by to stay with you."

"I don't want to put all of you out."

"You're not. I'm right where I want to be."

Jenny frowned. He wasn't making any sense. Brax must have seen her. He finished putting the last dish in the washer, then came over to stand next to her. He wrapped his hand around the nape of her neck, gently forcing her to look up at him.

"Haven't you figured it out, beautiful? I'm serious about you. I know you're not ready to hear this, and I'm more than willing to go slow. Consider me in first gear. We're friends who kiss. I want to build on that."

"Sex?" she squeaked out.

"Eventually." He grinned. "Is that really so scary?"

"Uhm. No?"

He laughed. "Love the enthusiasm, Babe."

She put her hands on his chest. "I'm sorry. I mean, yes?"

"Is sex so scary?" Brax teased.

"No, you big goof. Yes, eventually sex."

"It won't be sex. By the time we get to fourth gear, it'll be making love. But like I said, we have all the time in the world."

Jenny felt the steady beat of his heart under her palms, and her breasts ached and her core melted. "It better be sooner than that," she whispered.

"We'll see. Now let's get you back to the couch. Do you need ice on the ribs, or heat?"

Jenny thought about it. "Heat."

"Okay, then."

"But don't think you're getting out of telling me everything you know."

"It's not much, but I'll tell you everything," he promised.

How in the hell was he so lucky? He hated paperwork, and somehow, he was stuck with the gear accountability report for the month. What in the hell had he done to deserve this nightmare? Oh yeah, he'd requested PTO on the day everybody had to beat their obstacle course records. According to Linc, that was hell. Kostya must be getting them ready for another mission.

Brax had already tallied everything he'd needed when he went to the armory, now it was just a matter of inputting it into the computer. Gideon had laughed at him for not putting it into the tablet in the first place, thereby skipping a step. He was probably right, but trying to fill out those little columns and rows on the computer as he was accounting for everything was just asking for errors. Brax preferred his method, even if it took a little longer.

So far, everything was coming out perfect. That was because Nolan was responsible for gathering all of the gear at the end of each mission. Nolan was as OCD as they came when it came to the job, and thank God for it.

"You almost done?" Mateo asked as he popped his head over the cubicle where Brax was working.

"I need fifteen or twenty more minutes."

"You would have been done already if you would have just—"

"I don't want to hear it."

Mateo shrugged. "We're going to Marti's Grill for a beer. You in?"

Brax considered it. CiCi was at his house with Jenny,

and the idea of talking to some of his teammates sounded good. "Yeah, I'm in."

"See you there," Mateo said. Then he was gone.

Brax finished up in twenty minutes, but before he closed down his computer, Kostya came around the corner. "How are you doing?"

"Fine. Everything came out perfect."

"No big surprise. I'm going to hate it if Nolan ends up leaving to work for Simon in Jasper Creek."

Brax chuckled. "Yeah. Just don't put Ryker in charge, then you'll be all right."

Kostya nodded in agreement. "How's it going with Jenny?"

"Fine."

Kostya didn't respond, at least not verbally. He just raised his eyebrow.

"Is this a counseling session?"

"Do you need a counseling session?" Kostya asked.

"I was thinking of doing it over beers tonight, but this might be better. It's killing me that someone is out after Jenny."

Kostya came in further into the cubicle and leaned against the side of the desk. "Understandable. Is that all?"

Brax shook his head. "You know I've been talking to her every day since she got out of the hospital, right?"

Kostya nodded.

"I'm in deep. She's something else. Strong. Funny. She has a big heart, and cares about a lot of people. But she doesn't let people in. She doesn't believe that people will be there for her."

"What's her background? What's her story?"

"She'll tell me about college, but nothing sooner than that. Oh, she told me she's from Kaycee, Wyoming and confirmed both of her parents are dead. I think it has a population of three. Anyway, she let it slip once that dealing with the guards in Bangladesh was easier than dealing with her dad. When I tried to follow up, she shut down, so I know it had to be bad."

"What did she tell you about college?"

"She only has one friend from college, her old roommate, but she hasn't even reached out to her since she's been back in the States. It's weird."

"Sounds like a tough nut to crack, but if she's talked to you so much, you must have broken through."

"Yeah, but I don't want it to be just because I was the one that she associates with having rescued her. You know?"

"I see your point. But the woman you're describing isn't who Lark has described to me. She did say she was reticent. But Jenny opened up. Smiled. Laughed. Was easy to talk to. Seems to me that whatever she was like in the past, maybe her captivity has changed her."

Brax felt a weight lift off his shoulders. "That's really good to hear."

"What's your gut telling you?" Kostya asked.

"I know what my dick is telling me."

Kostya chuckled. "I'm sure you do."

"My gut's telling me that she wants something, but she needs to be coaxed. Not pushed. Just coaxed."

"That sounds right. Talk to Nolan. Out of everyone, Maggie was the one who needed to be coaxed. She came from a world of hurt growing up, and learning how to believe in something different was tough for her, but Nolan got through."

That was a good idea. Brax nodded. "Thanks."

"Are you heading to Marti's Grill?" Kostya asked.

"I think I'll pass. I want to get home."

"Understood."

19

Jenny couldn't believe it. All of her employee access was still live through the company web portal. Why hadn't they cut her off? Hell, it hadn't even occurred to her to try to access the company information until just now.

She was going to have to be damned careful to make sure nobody could see that she was accessing the information, especially her email. She bit her thumbnail.

"Stop it," she whispered harshly.

It was her third night at Brax's house, and despite the great bed and beautiful room, she was going stir crazy. At least she had been. Now that she'd found out she had access to the company's internal server, she was over the moon. Maybe now she could find out who was after her.

First and foremost, she didn't want to do anything that would tip off her company that she was logged-in and looking around. She pulled up her chat and pinged Jada.

JENNY: *Jada, can you give me a call tomorrow morning? I just realized I have access to my company's web portal, and I want to look around without having them realize I'm online.*

Jenny toggled over to the web portal and looked at the welcome page and then her chat pinged.

Jada: *That's great. Do you want me to call now?*
Jenny: *Why aren't you asleep?*
Jada: *Working on a project for Kane McNamara. Answer your phone.*

JENNY IMMEDIATELY PICKED up the phone when she saw Jada's name come up.

"That was fast." Jada said.

"Yeah, well, I'm really hoping you can do something. I don't know what. But something."

"Oh yeah, we can. Once I see who has been emailing you, I can backtrack into their email, hell, I'll have keys to the kingdom."

"You will?"

"Absolutely," Jada crowed. "This is going to be fun. Can you give me your username and password?"

"Sure." Jenny rattled it off and listened as Jada typed.

"Okay, I'm in."

"Aren't they going to see it's me?"

"Just for a moment. I'm switching over as a ghost,

that way I can dig deep into their system and see their back end. What I want to do is get into different people's email."

"You can do that?"

"Oh yeah. I should have thought about this right from the get-go. Too many times companies forget to cancel out their employee's web access. I should have been doing this as soon as you were shoved in front of the car. Damned wedding prep. If it weren't for my family, I wouldn't be so immersed in everything. My dad set aside money for my wedding. Even though he's not alive to give me away, he would expect me to have the wedding of the century. I have five older brothers who are making sure this happens. As it stands, things have totally gotten out of hand."

Jenny's stomach clenched. She couldn't imagine having a family like that, let alone a dad who would love her that much. It seemed surreal.

"That sounds wonderful," Jenny whispered.

"It's a pain in my ass, is what it is," Jada muttered. "Anyway, give me tonight, and I'll report back to you tomorrow."

"That would be great."

"Sleep tight."

Jada hung up.

Now Jenny was too jazzed to sleep. She put down her tablet, threw back the covers, and got out of bed. Maybe a snack would help her sleep. Okay, maybe not, but dammit, it sounded good. What's more, Brax had a great pantry, it was filled with good stuff. It was amazing that he was as fit as he was.

Brax kept the house at a nice temperature, so she didn't need to put on socks before she left her bedroom. She wasn't all that surprised when Faith met her in the kitchen.

"Shhhh. Don't wake Brax, okay?"

Faith let out a quiet *Woof*. Good to know she understood her. Now to find something good to eat that might help her sleep as well. She opened up the pantry and found tea.

"Ugh." She'd had enough tea while she'd worked in Bangladesh to last her a lifetime. Then she spied the container of powdered chocolate milk. "Hot damn."

Woof.

"Shhh." Faith let out another quiet *Woof*, and Jenny crouched down and rubbed her head. She stood back up and saw a box of dog treats in the pantry. She pulled one out and gave it to Faith, then she took out the container of hot chocolate.

She hip-checked the pantry door and immediately regretted it as pain zinged through her ribs.

"Dammit!"

"What did you do?" Brax asked in a husky voice.

Jenny whirled around and clutched the canister tight to her chest. "Fuck!"

"Baby, would you stop hurting yourself?" He reached out and gently pulled the canister out of her arms. "Looks like you found CiCi's stash. Why don't you go sit down and I'll make you a mug?"

"Because there is no way you'll put in nearly enough powder."

"Sure I will." He looked at the can. "It says two tablespoons to six fluid ounces."

"Exactly my point. I want chocolate-chocolate hot chocolate." Jenny reached for the canister.

"Tell me what you mean, and I'll do it."

She sighed. "Okay, you fill up the mug halfway with water, then microwave it til it's boiling, then you scoop in heaping tablespoons of mix until the mug is almost to the brim. That's chocolate-chocolate hot chocolate."

Brax stood there and stared down at her. "You're kidding, right?"

"No, I'm not."

"Nobody would do that."

"How often do you have to buy this stuff for CiCi?"

"Probably every other month."

"How many times does she come over?"

"Twice a month," Brax answered.

"And she always has hot chocolate, doesn't she."

Brax frowned. "How did you know?"

"I've been to the coffee shop with her. I've heard her order. I know how many pumps of chocolate syrup she asks for."

He reached out and stroked his knuckles down her cheek and she shivered. "I'm all for that for both of you. I get worried that you've both been through traumatic events and you could afford to put on some weight. So again, why don't you sit down, and I'll make you chocolate-chocolate hot chocolate?"

"That'd be great."

"How big of a mug do you want?"

"Not too much. Six ounces of water is just fine."

"Gotcha. Now go take a seat on the couch, and don't forget to wrap up in the throw blanket."

"I'm not cold, it's fine. Plus, I'll be hot once I start drinking the hot chocolate."

She spun around and headed for the living room.

LORD HAVE MERCY. She might be fine without a blanket, but I'm going to burst into flames watching her in that lacy tank top and those pajama shorts. She might need hot chocolate, but I'm going to need something a whole hell of a lot stronger.

He pulled down a mug and poured some water into it, then put it in the microwave. While he waited for that to heat, he grabbed a short glass and his good bottle of bourbon. He poured himself a healthy couple of shots. Thank God he'd thrown on a pair of jeans. If he'd been wearing a pair of sweats his hard-on would've been as obvious as Pinocchio's nose when he was lying.

The microwave dinged and he pulled out the mug of hot water, then proceeded to follow Jenny's instructions. He looked down at the thick goo. This couldn't be right. He took a sip and winced. She was going to fall into a sugar coma for sure.

He walked out to the living room with the two drinks and handed her the mug. Brax sat down in the armchair next to the couch where she was sitting. He saw her frown, but it was definitely for the best. After all, they were still in first gear.

"You're not going to sit next to me?"

"I'm fine over here."

Her frown deepened. If he wasn't mistaken, he saw a look of hurt flash over her face. He set down his glass on the coffee table, got up, and wrapped the blanket around Jenny.

"Now I can sit next to you."

"Oh." She blushed. As he sat down next to her and picked up his drink, she snuggled next to him. "You know, maybe you need to go put on a shirt."

Her cheek rubbed against his chest hair and Brax held back a groan. This was such a bad idea. He sucked down a large swallow of bourbon and Jenny giggled.

"You know, it's not nice to laugh at someone who's suffering."

"What are you talking about? I'm the one who's suffering," she said as she looked up at him. "Here I was minding my own business, just making a mug of chocolate sludge, and you come in half naked. I'd say I'm the one who has the right to protest."

Brax liked the way her sass came out in a husky tone. Yep, she was just as caught up in the molten moment as he was.

"Be quiet and drink your chocolate sludge," he whispered.

She took a sip of her hot chocolate and let out a satisfied sigh that had his cock twitching with excitement. For fuck's sake, he was thirty-two years old, why in the hell couldn't he get his body under control?

Jenny continued to sip, and he continued to twitch. At least she wasn't rubbing her face against his chest anymore. But then she moved. He knew it was just to get more comfortable because of her ribs, but it put her hip right against his thigh. Her hip that wasn't covered by the blanket. He could see her silky-smooth skin and it was killing him. He took another sip of bourbon. Why hadn't he poured himself a bigger drink?

"What are you drinking?"

"Bourbon."

"Oh. I think I like that. Can I try?"

Brax held out his left hand to take her mug, then handed her his glass of bourbon. He watched as she took a small sip. She wrinkled her nose as she held the alcohol in her mouth, then swallowed.

Once again, she gave him a satisfied sigh. "I like the burn."

That was it. He was done. Brax snatched the glass from her and slammed that and the mug on the coffee table, then turned to her. "Second gear. Tonight, we're going for second gear. Tell me if I do anything that hurts your ribs."

She gave him a radiant smile. "You could never hurt me." She reached out for him and the blanket slipped to the floor. Brax hauled her up into his lap. Her cute ponytail had to go. He slipped off the hair scrunchie, then he carefully splayed the fingers of one hand through the silky strands as he moved her head so that her mouth was at the perfect angle for the perfect kiss.

Dipping his head, he pressed his lips against her barely parted lips. Brax took his time, sipping, stroking, and coaxing her lips to part for him. Enticing her to play was part of the fun, and he wasn't going to skimp on any part of his time with Jenny Rivers.

When her lips parted and he felt her fingernails dig into his nape, he slicked his tongue along her lower lip. Chocolate had never tasted so good as it did on Jenny's lips. When he felt her tongue touch his, he shivered. He pulled her closer, careful of her ribs, he cradled her in his arms and deepened the kiss.

Jenny let out a soft mew like a kitten would make and she trembled. Her response ratcheted up Brax's level of need, but he tried to hold it back. He'd promised her slow. She'd just gotten out of the hospital.

Jenny snaked her hand around to his front and was soon spearing her fingers through his chest hair until she scraped the nub of his nipple with her fingernail. He thrust his tongue deep inside her mouth, and she pulled his head down harder.

God, she's going to burn me up.

Their tongues tangled for long moments, and Brax felt lost. Every thought of how he wanted things to go flew out of his head; instead, he was swept up in a world of glorious sensation. He didn't know when his hand had moved, but he was stroking the soft skin of her back underneath her tank top. How could someone who felt so delicate have survived so much?

Jenny yanked her mouth away from his. Before he could protest the loss, she was at his chest, her greedy tongue sweeping circles around his nipple. His head fell back against the couch.

"Christ!"

She stopped and he felt Jenny's smile against his

chest. Then she continued with her torture, and he let her. It was too good to stop, but finally his befuddled mind kicked in and wanted to join the game.

Second gear.

As Jenny played, he tugged at her tank top and pushed it up so that it rested above her breasts. He couldn't get a good view with her pressed against his chest, but that didn't matter. Now he could feel. Following up on a favorite fantasy, he cupped both of her breasts in his hands, and lightly brushed his thumbs over her distended nipples.

"Ahhhh," Jenny moaned.

Yep, two could play at this game. He continued with his torture, but soon realized that Jenny wouldn't be stopped. She was soon grazing her teeth along his pebbled flesh, trying to make him lose his mind. But dammit, he was a SEAL, and he was trained to withstand torture.

Brax gently kneaded her plump breasts as he continued to skim his thumbs against her nipples, but soon it was too much. He had to see her. He had to.

He was easily able to twist and then Jenny was lying on the sofa, looking up at him.

"How'd you do that?"

"Superior upper body strength."

"That's no fair. I wasn't done yet," Jenny protested.

"I wanted to watch what I was doing," he whispered into the night.

He watched her green eyes give him a considering look, then she smiled. "Only for a little bit, then I want to go back to what I was doing."

"I'm sure you can find something to do from this position," he teased.

Brax lowered his gaze from her face, downward to her breasts. God, she was gorgeous. He'd been wondering ever since the wakey-wakey song what color her nipples were, and now he knew. They were a rosy pink and meant to be pleasured. By him. Only by him.

20

The heat of Brax's gaze made Jenny squirm.

"Touch me," she begged.

"Patience. I'm getting there."

"Well, get there faster."

He looked back up into her eyes. "We're still taking this slow. I want to make sure we do this right, Jenny. You're too important to me to get this wrong."

"The only way you can get this wrong is by not touching me. I'm dying here." And she was. She'd never been so turned on in her life. Hell, she didn't know it was possible to be this turned on. Yeah, she'd watched sexy movies, and some of the books she'd read were romantic and hot, but this was a whole other universe.

"Jenny, I've lost you. Where'd you go?"

"Brax, being with you is like being in a world where only sensation exists. The heat of your gaze, the feel of your hands on my hips, the rasp of your beard on my cheeks, every little thing has me turned inside out. I was made for this moment with you."

Jenny watched as his eyes dilated.

"I don't know what to say." His voice was the wash of sand over velvet, raspy and heartfelt.

"Don't say anything. Just know that there isn't anything that we could do tonight that wouldn't be beautiful and divine. I have never known anyone like you. Your honor shines through everything you do. I love how every word and touch you give me makes me feel adored."

Brax rested his forehead on hers. "I'm glad," he whispered. "It's true. I do adore you, Jenny."

"Please know, I want to be here for you, just like you've been here for me. I want to be your equal in this and in all things. I want you to know you're adored. Do you?" Jenny couldn't help the quiver in her voice.

He looked at her. Really looked at her, and she knew that he saw just how big of a leap she was taking.

"I love you, Jenny," he said, then he kissed her forehead.

"Then please make love to me."

"Gladly."

HER WORDS unlocked feelings that had been trapped deep inside him for decades. Feelings Brax hadn't even known were a missing part of him. It was as if Jenny had found the way to the center of his heart and enclosed it with love and light. No longer did he feel like someone would leave him on a whim. Instead he found someone who would stay and fight the good fight with him. He knew this woman. He knew she had her demons that she still hadn't told him about, but Jenny was still willing to unite with him going forward. He knew her strength. She would keep her promise, and for the first time in decades, Brax felt whole.

He stood up and gazed down at Jenny as the soft lamplight painted her skin in gold. She smiled up at him. Soon he was carrying her to his bed. He pushed back the covers and laid her down.

He had to ask one more time. "Are you sure?"

"I'm sure." Jenny's arms beckoned him, but he ignored them. Instead, he pulled her sleep shorts off her body and grinned.

"We might even get to fifth gear tonight," he teased.

"Well, you *are* a SEAL."

"I'm glad you understand."

Slowly he readjusted her position so that her legs fell off the bed and he was able to kneel between them.

"Oh my God. Brax," she wailed. "This is so much more than fifth gear. Couldn't we dial it back?"

"Just lie back and think of England or something. Isn't that what they did in the olden days?" Brax could see the glimmering dew on the lips of her sex, but he wanted to make sure she was a lot more ready before they made love. Jenny had only talked about her college boyfriend and that had been a long time ago.

Then there was the added pleasure of tasting this beautiful woman. Watching her tremble with her release. Yes, this was something he was looking forward to on so many different levels. Brax traced the seam of her sex and Jenny bucked up. His woman was sensitive.

He did it again, and again, and again.

"Brax." Her whisper was so soft he barely heard it. But he did.

They had a long way to go. A whisper was nowhere good enough. He smiled to himself. He parted her sex with his thumbs and admired the pink beauty within. Her clitoris peeked out, almost ready. He swiped his tongue to catch the silky essence of her desire.

"Brax." Her whisper, louder.

He could hear both disquiet and pleasure in her voice, and now he had a goal. Soon she would only feel pleasure. He continued to softly lick and listen to her breathless cries, and when one hand grasped his short hair and pushed down, triumph rushed through him. He circled her engorged clit with his tongue.

"It's too much," Jenny cried out.

It wasn't nearly enough.

He continued with his torture until he sucked the little morsel into his mouth, reveling in the incoherent cries coming from his lover. He pierced her entrance with a finger, and she welcomed him with a tight, warm grasp and a high shriek of pleasure as she crashed into the peak of orgasm.

Brax got up and moved her so that they could lie side by side on the bed. He needed to hold his woman. Jenny cuddled closer. In his eagerness to pull her tight, he almost forgot about her injured ribs, but he stopped himself in time.

He loved her fast, soft breaths that tickled his chest hair. He stroked her pretty brown hair away from her face.

"Kiss me," she murmured.

"I'll taste like—"

"I don't care. I love us together. And anyway, I'm soon going to be tasting you," she grinned.

Brax thought his cock might push through his zipper at the promise of Jenny's pillow-soft lips sucking him to orgasm.

By the time they were done kissing, Jenny was squirming against him. She wrenched her head away from his, and her hand cupped his crotch. "Please tell me you have condoms."

"I have condoms."

"Thank God."

He was done questioning this beautiful woman. Jenny knew what she wanted, and he damn sure knew what he wanted. He got up and went to the bathroom to grab protection, then he came back to find Jenny propped up on her elbows, watching him.

"Well?"

"I've got them." He held up the packets, then tossed them on the nightstand.

"That's not what I meant. When are you going to show me the goods, Sailor?"

Brax threw back his head and laughed. "Curious much?"

"Yep. Now strip."

He was still chuckling when he shucked his jeans. He stood up straight and waited for her assessment. He didn't have to wait long.

"And all along you call *me* beautiful? You've got it all wrong, Brax."

Am I blushing?

He put one knee on the bed and both hands on either side of her head, trapping her. "We're done with talking," he said softly.

"I understand why you don't want to talk. With so much of your blood supporting your erection, how can you possibly carry on a conversation?" Her eyes twinkled.

He dipped down and softly bit her bottom lip.

She grabbed at his head when he reared back.

"I want more kisses," Jenny protested.

"And you'll get some. First, I think your breasts need some attention."

Brax tried to go slow. He did. He really did. But the moonlight gave her breasts a silver hue. First it had been gold, now silver. His woman was truly magical. He plumped up her right breast, then covered the swollen flesh with his mouth and sucked.

"Brax," Jenny moaned.

He knew she was thrashing her head, because he could feel her hair hitting the arm that was still supporting him. He kept up with his torture, then added the scrape of his teeth. Soft. Gentle. Then a little rough.

Jenny screamed. "More."

Brax was glad to provide.

What seemed like either a second or an eternity, he had to end their play. He needed more. When he looked up, he saw green eyes that mirrored his hunger and greed.

"Please say now. I can't wait anymore," Jenny begged.

He reached between her legs. She was drenched. She was ready.

"Now, beautiful. I promise, now."

Brax tore open the condom and sheathed himself, conscious of Jenny's avid gaze. As he positioned himself against her tender flesh he started to sweat.

Slow.

Slow.

She'd been so tight. He knew that this could be painful for her, no matter what she might have said.

"Stop fooling around," she growled.

Damn. This woman. Is there any wonder that he adored her?

He watched her face as he pressed inward. All he saw was want. He pushed in farther and his whole body began to tingle as her tight warmth squeezed him. But no matter what, he had to keep his head, this was all about Jenny. He could see her gaze turn inward as she concentrated on the sensations happening inside her body.

"Okay?" he gritted out the question.

She nodded her head. "More."

He pressed in another inch.

"I said more." Her words had a definite bite to them.

He delved deeper, then her nails bit into his back, and her legs encircled his waist, and he knew that she was right there with him.

"This is so good, Braxton. So good."

"It's about to get better," he promised.

He started a slow rhythm, still watching every expression that passed over her face. When she started to moan and tremble, he went faster...deeper...harder.

Jenny shouted out his name. "Brax, help me."

"I've got you."

"So close."

And she was. He worked his hand between their bodies and brushed his thumb over her clit. She cried out. It wasn't good enough. He needed relief, and so did she. Yeah, there was still a tiny bit of his brain able to concentrate on Jenny and her needs, but her beauty, want, and greed were like nothing he had ever experienced before. He knew that when he let go, he would never be the same.

"Brax," she whimpered.

"I've got you," he said again.

He pinched the slippery knot of nerves, and her arms, legs, and sheath clenched around him. He was lost. He drove deep and let out a shout that became her name. Over and over again his release pulsed, making him dizzy, scrambling his brain. It was only by sheer force of will that he stopped himself from falling on top of her. Instead, he rolled them so that he wouldn't injure her ribs, as his empty head hit the pillows.

He didn't know how long he stayed like that. His world distilled down to one thing. Jenny.

When the fog began to lift, he knew he needed a plan, because there was no way he was going to go through the rest of his life without her by his side.

21

Jenny moved Brax's arm, attempting to sneak out of bed.

"Where'ya going?"

"Just need to go to the bathroom," she lied.

"'Kay."

He rolled over and went back to sleep. She wasn't surprised. It wasn't so much the fact that they had made love three times the night before, but she knew how on edge he had been since the attempt on her life. He'd hardly been getting any sleep. It amazed her that he'd been asleep last night when she'd gotten up with Faith.

So far Brax had done all of the cooking, but this morning she wanted to surprise him. It wasn't that she couldn't cook, it was just that her job kept her so busy that cooking a meal for herself was usually the last thing on her mind.

She headed to her bedroom and put on leggings and a long tee, then went to the bathroom across the hall and washed up, did her business, and brushed her teeth. Back to her bedroom, she took her phone off the nightstand. It still had a pretty good charge, which she'd need to find the perfect recipes for special breakfast dishes. After all, she'd have to work with what Brax had on hand. She absently patted Faith's head as she headed to the kitchen.

"You were a good girl last night, weren't you?"

She found Faith's food and filled up her bowl, added water to her water bowl, then checked out Brax's fridge and pantry. She started scrolling through fancy French toast recipes until she found one that would work with what she had on hand.

"Perfect," she mumbled.

Even after using the four eggs necessary for the casserole, there would be plenty left over for the egg dish she intended to bake. Jenny grinned. After all of Brax's hard work last night, the least she could do was reward the man.

Whoops!

She leaned against the counter. How in the hell could she get all tingly and achy just by thinking of what they had done? Her stomach clenched again.

Whew-wee. That man was powerful, even when he wasn't near.

She giggled, then stood back up straight. Time to get cooking.

Brax rolled over and reached out for Jenny, only to find her side of the bed cool. *What the hell? She said she would be right back, hadn't she?* Brax shook his head, trying to clear the cobwebs.

Damn, last night had been something else. The phone on his nightstand vibrated again. That must have been what woke him. He snatched it up and looked at the display. It was Gideon.

"Good morning," he said, then promptly yawned.

"You sound tired. I would have thought that by taking time off, you would be more rested."

"I've been fixing things up around the house. It's been hard work."

"Are you sure that's the only thing that has you tired?" Gideon asked.

Brax frowned. "What's with all the questions?"

"Just wondering if Jenny is tired this morning, too."

"Don't tell me you geniuses have a bet going on as to when we'll sleep together. That's just wrong."

"Seems to me you won the bet about Ryker and Amy, so I don't know why you're bitching. Now spill."

"A gentleman doesn't kiss and tell. Now why are you calling?"

"Jada and I want to come over. We have some information and some questions for Jenny."

"Tell me first."

"Jada won't let me. She tracked down a lot of it, based on information that Jenny gave her last night."

"What did Jenny tell Jada?"

"Just tell me, are we good to come over, or not?"

Brax rubbed his stubbled chin. "Yeah. It's good. But give us a half hour."

"That's how long it will take for us to get there, so you're good."

Brax hung up and grabbed the same pair of jeans he wore last night and yanked them on. It was time to find out what Jenny had been up to before he'd found her stealing chocolate from his pantry.

As soon as he opened the bedroom door, heavenly smells hit him. What in the hell were they?

"Jenny?"

"I'm in the kitchen."

"I figured that," he mumbled to himself.

When he got to the kitchen, he saw her in the process of taking one casserole pan out of the oven and putting another one in. She was doing it at the same time, one in each hand. He winced. He stopped short and didn't say a word so that she wouldn't drop one.

When she made the switch and closed the oven door with her hip, he spoke up.

"What in the hell do you think you are doing?"

She looked over her shoulder at him. "Cooking."

"How about doing it a little more carefully. You could have easily dropped one of those pans, and if it was the hot one, you would have been badly burned."

Jenny rolled her eyes. "Hold on there, Mr. SEAL, I've been cooking for myself since I was sixteen. I know what I'm doing. I'm a big girl."

"You're a big girl with cracked ribs. Are you even wearing your bandage?"

She bit her inner lip. "You know, you're a lot less

adorable when you're being overbearing. I'll grant you the bitching about the bandage, but cut it out about the pans. I know what I'm doing."

"When you're injured and not at full strength?" he asked in a softer tone of voice. He knew he'd blown it charging in like an asshole, but she'd scared him.

She blew the hair out of her face. "I see your point," she admitted. "But I don't appreciate the delivery."

He walked into the kitchen and brushed his knuckles over her flushed cheek, happy when she leaned into the caress. "I'm sorry, Jenny. You scared me. I don't like the idea of you being injured."

"Okay, I can see that. And you're probably right. I'll take it easier."

He sniffed the air. "Care to tell me what you made? It smells delicious."

"You didn't have challah bread, but the loaf of French bread you had was good in a pinch for this French toast casserole. Also, it calls for blueberries, but I used your strawberries."

"Good, I like strawberries," Brax said as he peered into the casserole pan and took a deep breath. What did you put into the oven?"

"That's a cheese and egg casserole with some crumbled bacon."

"Thank God, Jada and Gideon are coming over. There is no way we could have made a dent in all this food."

"I would have screwed up the recipes if I tried to cut them in half. I suck at math."

He kissed her self-deprecating smile. Then kissed her deeper for good measure.

She pushed him away. "When are they going to be here?"

He glanced at the clock on the microwave. "About twenty minutes from now."

"I need to shower. Keep your kisses to yourself. Can you take the eggs out of the oven when the timer rings?"

"Aye-aye."

He watched as she hustled down the hallway, then pulled a fork out of the silverware drawer and took a big bite out of the French toast casserole and groaned.

So good.

JENNY GAVE Jada a hug when she came through the door. She still didn't feel comfortable enough with Gideon to do the same. He must have sensed it, because he didn't offer one.

"Come on into the kitchen, Jenny has cooked up a feast."

"You cooked?" Jada asked. "What's that?"

Jenny giggled. "I just threw a couple of things into the oven. It was no big deal."

"Wait til you taste them. It's a big deal." Brax grinned.

Jenny noticed that Gideon brought his tablet into the kitchen with him, and Jada carried her beautiful leather purse with her as well. Weird.

Brax pointed to Gideon's tablet. "No work during breakfast. We're going to savor this meal, got it?"

Gideon's lip twitched. "Got it." He sat down and turned his tablet upside down on the kitchen table. Jada put her purse down underneath the table. Now that Jenny thought about it, she'd bet that her purse contained her tablet as well.

"Did you find something out with my username and password?" Jenny asked.

"Uh-uh-uh," Brax admonished. "Food first, then talk. I've been dying to try this."

"What are you talking about? I saw how much of the casserole was gone before I put it in your serving dish. You devoured at least two pieces."

"What can I say, I worked hard last night."

Jada snickered.

"Shut up, already," Jenny said as she rolled her eyes. Brax took a big scoop of the eggs, then passed the dish to Jada whose eyes widened.

"You made this?" she asked Jenny.

"Sure."

"This is like something from a restaurant." She took a big scoop. Not as big as Brax's, but big. They passed around both dishes, and the bowl of melons that Brax had cut up. Pretty soon everybody was quiet as they dug into their food.

Jenny was itching to hear what Jada found out, so she'd taken just a little bit of the food and was done first.

"So, Jada—" she started.

"Not done," Brax said.

"You don't know what I was going to talk about," Jenny protested. "I wanted to know where she got her purse. It is crazy cute. I want to see what else they have."

Jada looked up and grinned. "I got it online. Kate Spade. Love their stuff. You need to shop their outlet. Lots of deals to be had."

"I'm going to be on their site today."

"Oh God, not another one," Gideon groaned. "Please don't say you like shoes," the man begged.

"Sure, I like shoes." Jenny smiled. She turned to Jada. "You, too?"

"Oh, do I ever. That was one of the worst and best things about the house blowing up. I lost all my shoes. But then I got to start replacing them all. The insurance adjuster had a hard time believing how much all of my shoes were worth."

Gideon shook his head. "*I* had a hard time believing how much those shoes cost. Shit, Jada, you could have bought a new car for the price of all of those shoes."

She looked over at her fiancé and batted her eyes. "A small economy car. One of those ones without the backseat." She turned back to Jenny. "Let me know when you want to go shopping. I'm there."

"Uhm, I'm not sure that you and I are on the same wavelength when it comes to shoe shopping. I'm thinking about a collection that will equal the amount of a used laptop. You know, maybe a five-year-old used laptop."

"I knew there was a reason I liked you," Brax crowed.

"You lucky bastard," Gideon muttered.

"Oh, quit your complaining. You have never had to pay for anything of mine, you big oaf. My consulting gigs are making money hand over fist, and you know it."

Jenny was impressed with the pride in Jada's voice.

Gideon reached over and put his arm around Jada's shoulder, then tugged her close for a kiss. "You are amazing. Have I told you that lately?" he asked quietly.

"You forgot to this morning, so thank you," she whispered back. "Love you, Gideon."

He gave her a light kiss. "Love you more."

22

Brax had insisted on clearing the breakfast dishes, and Gideon helped.

"You cooked, I clean. Them's the rules," Brax said.

"I like him," Jada whispered when the two men were in the kitchen. "Actually, I love him for saving Lucy's life. But I like him for you."

Jenny frowned. "You do? Why?"

"I've seen him with two women since Gideon and I have been together. They didn't last long, but he never seemed to be as emotionally invested as he is with you. When he looks at you, it's like you've hung the moon."

"Really?"

"Really."

Jada pulled her purse into her lap, then grabbed her tablet. "It was great you gave me your username and password, but it turned out I didn't need it. Gideon had already found a way into your company's intranet, and he'd hacked into everybody's email that he thought was relevant. Like I said, my brain hasn't been firing on all cylinders because of the wedding. I feel like a fool."

"Jada, don't feel that way. Take my advice and enjoy it. Being surrounded by your family's love is a blessing. You're lucky."

She looked up at Jenny. "You weren't?"

Jenny shook her head.

"What happened?"

Brax and Gideon came back into the room.

"It was nothing," Jenny whispered. "I'm more interested in what you and Gideon found out."

"What was nothing?" Brax asked.

Damn, the man didn't miss a thing.

"Just girl talk. Shopping. You wouldn't be interested," Jenny said quickly. Brax gave her a long look, but let it go. She knew he was going to circle back later.

Shit.

Gideon sat down next to Jada, and he turned over his tablet. He pulled up some information, then turned it around so that she and Brax could see his screen.

"Jenny, who is Fiona?" Gideon asked.

She frowned. "Fiona? What does she have to do with anything?"

"Can you just tell us?" Jada asked in a calm voice. "We found something in the Vice President of HR's email, where he mentioned the name Fiona and your name, Jennifer Rivers. He'd deleted the email, but didn't bother to empty his trash."

"What did the email say?" Jenny asked.

"Baby, first tell them about Fiona. Isn't she a friend of yours?" Brax asked.

She looked over at him and nodded. "Yes, she is." She turned back to Gideon and Jada. "Fiona Richards is someone who started out as a temp in our London office while I was working there. She eventually ended up as the executive assistant to the Director of Operations and the Director of Finance. Normally there was one EA for the five Directors in the C-Suite, but she'd gone out on maternity leave. So, they had to get two temps, Fiona and Angela."

"I got her personnel file," Gideon said.

"Yeah, and I went over it with a fine-tooth comb," Jada nodded. "It was slim, because she was a temp. It says that the two directors she reported to were considering hiring her on in a fulltime capacity, but one day her temp agency called them and said she wasn't going to return. It was a black eye on the temp agency, and the two directors were pissed. The agency lost their contract with Cyber Tech. It was weird. Gideon and I looked everywhere through the HR records to see if she had reported some kind of harassment that might have been a reason for her to leave, but there was nothing."

"I hacked PeopleNow, her agency, and there is no record of a Fiona Richards ever having worked there. None. What's even more interesting is that so far, we've been unable to track down Fiona anywhere in London. Three weeks after her disappearance, you were transferred to Bangladesh. Can you tell us why this might have happened?"

"I had put in my request for a new assignment two months before Fiona quit. I don't think that the two things are related. As for Fiona and my name being linked by the VP of HR here in the States, that doesn't make any sense."

"But you know something about her disappearance, don't you," Jada prompted.

Jenny nodded. "She was in an untenable situation. It was worse than sexual harassment if you could believe it."

"What was it, Honey?" Brax asked as he put his arm around her shoulders.

"Fiona was pretty. Actually she was…is beautiful. Curves in all the right places. Blonde. She loves to wear these vintage suits to the office, that really show off all of her assets. She gets them from secondhand shops, so they're cheap, and she looked great in them. I think Dave chose her as their EA because of how she looked, and Edgar chose her because he thought she was stupid."

"Was she?" Brax asked.

"Fiona couldn't put down that she had a degree, because she didn't, but she was taking night classes, and only had one more class to take to get her degree in mathematics. It was actuarial mathematics."

Gideon whistled. "She could probably run circles on the Finance Director," Gideon chuckled.

"That was the problem. Six months into her gig, she realized that he was moving money around into a shell corporation. What's worse, he had opened it up in her name."

"How in the hell had he done that?" Jada demanded to know. "She should have been smarter than that."

"Fiona and I pieced it together later on. Edgar supposedly broke his foot the first month she started, and couldn't come into the office for four weeks. There were small things that needed to be signed and notarized, that he authorized her to do on his behalf. He'd say he'd read it over at home, and she'd print it out and sign it in front of the notary. Easy."

Jada groaned. "She might have been school smart, but not street smart. He ate her for lunch."

"Yep," Jenny nodded.

"He pulled this in the first couple of months she worked there. That must have been the point she signed the corporation papers and the bank account under her name. But of course, Edgar had all the access to the account."

"Of course," Jada said.

"So, four months later when she finds out that over two million pounds have been embezzled from the company, she traced it back to Edgar. Then she realizes all the money has been deposited into an account in her name. She's screwed. By that time, we had become friends, and she tells me what has happened."

"Why would you believe her?" Gideon asked.

"You have to know her background to believe her. We had a girl's night at my apartment one night and exchanged war stories."

"War stories?" Brax asked.

"Our childhoods. Hers won. She had documentation. She showed me the articles on the internet. Her dad killed her mother, then held Fiona and her little sister hostage for ten hours before killing himself. Her dad was a thief, and the cops had been closing in on him. Her mom was trying to leave with Fiona and her sister, before the cops raided the place. There is no way that Fiona would ever steal anything."

Jenny looked around and saw that everybody was nodding.

"So, Fiona did a runner?" Brax said. "Do you know where she is?"

Jenny nodded. "She changed her identity, got new papers, and is currently living in Spain. She speaks fluent Spanish, so she's fine. She wants to hire someone to clear her name and bring Edgar to justice, but I haven't talked to her since my kidnapping."

"Did you ever email Fiona?" Gideon asked.

"Sure, we worked together. But I didn't contact her at all after she left, or after she told me what was going on. I didn't want any kind of communication going on between the two of us."

"How about when you were in Bangladesh?" Brax asked.

"Only from a new Gmail account that I made up just to talk to her."

"That won't work," Gideon said. "You still have to point back to other email accounts for backup."

Jenny frowned. "Yeah, you're right. But would the company be watching my email?"

"Did you email from your company computer?" Gideon asked.

"No, I did it from my private computer." Jenny grinned.

"Did you do it from work, when you were connected to the company internet?" Jada asked.

Jenny nodded.

"You're hosed."

"So do you think Jenny being shoved in the street could be due to this thing in London?" Brax asked.

"Could be," Gideon said slowly. "The other wildcard is that the VP of Public Relations, Roy Jeckel, was fired three weeks ago after thirty-five years. When I read through his HR file, it was clear that the company set him up as the fall guy for the bad PR surrounding the Jenny scandal."

"That wasn't his fault. It wasn't his decision not to pay my ransom," Jenny protested.

"Yeah, but they're saying it's his fault for all the bad press and their plunging stock price," Jada said.

"Assholes," Jenny muttered.

"There you go. We have a couple of people who are suspects. Edgar and Roy," Jada said.

"Edgar has no reason to come after Jenny. He doesn't know about her connection to Fiona," Brax argued.

"If the VP of HR here in the States mentioned the two of them in the same email, then I'd say they've been connected," Gideon disagreed.

Jenny shivered. "I was supposed to be safe when I got back to America."

"You will be, Honey. I promise."

Brax pulled her closer and kissed the top of her head. She hoped he was right.

23

"I suppose I have to tell Kostya you're taking more personal time?" Gideon said to Brax as the two men watched Jada showing Jenny a website on her tablet.

"Is that going to be a problem?"

"No. I think Kostya has forgotten to put down that you've been off the last couple of days, so you've got more than you think." Gideon grinned.

Damn, I'm a lucky bastard.

"What's your gut telling you?" Brax asked his second-in-command.

"I don't think it's the PR guy. He's got thirty-five years with the company. He's just a guy out of a job, not a real good reason to kill someone."

"Yeah. That's my take too," Brax agreed. "But how did this guy from London track her down? And wouldn't it be more likely that they would want her alive so they could find out where Fiona is?"

Gideon shrugged. "And for all we know, it could be

some freak who's taken a shine to her because she's been in the papers."

Brax groaned. "Why'd you even say that?"

"Because it's true. But right now, she should be safe, because nobody knows your address. There's no government paper trail, like there was when she was at the hotel."

"When you say that, it points to London again. Someone with a couple of million dollars to play with would be able to find things out, not some poor PR shmo, or some crazy fan."

"That's why I'm digging around there first. I'll get you the address of Roy Jeckel, and you and one of the guys can go check him out. Take Mateo."

Brax looked over his shoulder at Jenny.

"If you're worried about her, let's get her over to my house," Gideon said. "After the last incident, I've got it wired every which way from Sunday to make sure I'll know if there are any intruders. It's a fortress. She can stay with Jada."

"Yeah, that'd be good."

"Of course, Jenny is going to end up spending hundreds, if not thousands, of dollars."

"Hopefully it will spur her on to sue Cyber Tech. Those bastards shouldn't be able to get away with what they did."

"Amen," Gideon agreed.

"So, WHAT ARE THEY DOING AGAIN?" Jenny asked Jada.

"Brax and Mateo are checking out Jeckel, and Gideon is over at Kane McNamara's house to see if they can find out more about Edgar."

"Who's Kane?"

"He's Gideon's counterpart in Night Storm. Night Storm is another SEAL Team."

"And Brax's team is called Omega Sky, right?"

Jada nodded. "I think we need to call Amy over. She could cook up some food while we shop."

"I can cook," Jenny protested.

"You're going to be too busy. I already called Leila and told her what to bring. I wanted to see how you'd look in a couple of outfits she had, so I could see what would look good on you before we order."

"Huh?" Jenny was definitely confused.

"Where's all your stuff?" Jada asked.

"My stuff?"

"Yeah, your stuff. Your things that you put into storage before you left for Bangladesh."

"I'd rented a furnished flat, because I knew my assignment was only going to last a year. I took what clothes I might need with me to Bangladesh. The work suits and stuff I just gave away when I left London. I have some things that I left in storage here in Virginia, but it was stuff I bought right out of college. There's nothing like what you're showing me."

"So we'll start from scratch." Jada grinned with anticipation.

"Jada, I have to warn you, I don't spend much on clothes. I'm a saver."

"We won't spend much. You just need some classic

pieces that you can add onto. You're going to be job hunting right?"

Jenny nodded.

"Then we need to look. And aren't you going to be going out with Brax?"

"He's a jeans and t-shirt kind of guy."

"I've seen him dress up. You're going to need a couple of dresses. I think with your coloring that autumn colors would look good on you. What do you think?"

"I think what I really need to do is call Tina and Fiona. I haven't called them since I got back to the States. If they saw what happened in the news, they were probably a bit worried." Jada got up and started backing away from the table.

"Okay, you do that. I'll call Amy and get some of my accessories that I think you might like. Too bad we're not the same shoe size."

Jenny fled to Gideon's study, then checked the time and realized it was the middle of the night in Spain, so she gave up on the idea of calling Fiona. Instead, she decided to dial Tina's number.

"Oh my God. You actually called!" Tina shrieked in her ear.

"Calm down."

"I will not calm down. I've been worried sick about you."

She'd really screwed up. She should have known that Tina would be worried about her. What had she been thinking?

"I'm sorry, Tina. But didn't you read that I was back in the States, safe and sound?"

"Don't give me that line of garbage. They said you were recovering from injuries. You'd been a hostage for three weeks. What did they do to you, Jenny?" Jenny's heart lurched when she heard Tina's whimper. Then Tina started to cry.

"Please don't cry. It's all okay. I'm fine. Everything's fine." Jenny didn't know how long she crooned different words while Tina calmed down. She finally heard her friend blow her nose.

"You're lying to me. You're not fine."

"Really, Tina I am."

"Three weeks. You were a hostage for three weeks, and then you had to go to the hospital. What happened? Please tell me."

Jenny couldn't say anything. There was no way she was going to tell her friend about the mud hut. "I wasn't abused, if that's what you're worried about. Nobody raped me."

"But they did other things, didn't they?" Tina persisted.

"Tina, it's over with. It's in the past."

"I need to come to you. I need to make sure you're all right. I'm taking the first plane to Virginia."

And then it clicked. Tina was much more than just a friend. Tina was the sister of her heart. How had she not realized that? Jenny felt a tear trickle down her cheek. How lucky was she?

"Where are you staying? What's the address? I'll rent a car when my plane lands."

"Tina, things are complicated right now. I promise I'll come and visit as soon as I can," Jenny soothed.

"Not good enough. I want to see you tomorrow." Tina was using her stubborn voice.

"About the address. I'm staying at someone's house for the time being."

"Fine, give me her address."

"Uhm, it's a man. He was one of the men on the team that rescued me..."

Tina didn't say anything, so Jenny pressed on. "There was something weird that happened a couple of days ago, and he wants to make sure I'm safe. Right now, I'm staying at his house."

Again, Tina was silent. Jenny couldn't stand it, and she looked down at her phone. The connection was live, so she plowed on.

"He's really nice. Protective too. You'd like him."

When Tina remained silent, Jenny couldn't stand it anymore. "Say something. Anything," she begged.

"Let me get this straight. Since you've been back in the States, something weird happened, i.e. something bad happened, and now one of the super soldiers who rescued you is protecting you by having you stay at his house. Do I have this right?"

"Uhm. Yeah."

"What the fuck happened?"

"I might have gotten pushed into oncoming traffic."

"What?" Tina screeched. "Somebody tried to kill you?"

"Kind of."

"And now this super soldier went all protective on your ass and has you tucked away at his house? Right?"

"Yeah, I guess so," Jenny winced.

"Another question. What does he look like?"

Jenny peeked around the corner and saw that Jada was still concentrating on her tablet. She was probably finding ways for Jenny to deplete her savings account. "He's hot."

"Have you fucked him?"

"God, Tina, I can't believe you just asked that."

"Well, have you?"

"We made love," Jenny finally admitted.

"Oh, that's so much worse," Tina wailed. "Are you in love with this guy? What's his name?"

"Brax. I don't think I'm in love with him." Jenny bit her thumbnail.

"That does it, I'm coming to visit. I can be there this weekend."

"No! It's not safe."

"What do you mean it's not safe?"

"We're still trying to figure out who tried to kill me. The men on his team are worried that they might try again. You need to stay in Colorado."

Tina was quiet and this time Jenny knew that she was processing everything. "You know you could just come here. You'd be safe. Nobody would know where you were. Lou's a big guy." Tina said, referring to her husband.

"Yes he is, but he's an accountant. I think I'll stick with Brax. Anyway, you're my best friend. They'd know. I'm safer with the SEALs."

"Your super soldier is a SEAL?"

"Yeah."

Tina sighed. "Well, okay. But don't you dare not call me again. I want to hear from you every day, otherwise I'm going to stalk your ass. You got it?"

Jenny giggled. "I've got it."

"I love you, Jenny," Tina said softly. "You make sure that Brax takes care of you, okay?"

"Okay."

Tina hung up and Jenny smiled.

How stupid have I been not talking to Tina more often? As soon as this bullshit is done, I'm flying out to Colorado and visiting her.

BRAX AND MATEO didn't have any luck at Jeckel's house in Chesapeake, so they drove out to Lake Anna where the man had a cabin.

"Pretty," Mateo said as they drove along the lakeshore.

"I was wondering, do you think Jase is going to retire?" Brax asked Mateo.

"Where'd that question come from?" Mateo sighed.

"I'm just thinking about this guy Jeckel, and how he lost his job after thirty-five years. Must have come as a blow. Then I thought about Jase."

"Jase is convinced that he'll get back to one hundred percent," Mateo answered. "We both know what a stubborn son of a bitch he is, so maybe he will."

Brax nodded. "But what if?"

"Well, what would you do?"

"I've been thinking about it. Nolan has that opportunity in Jasper Creek, working for the Lieutenant Commander. I'd check out something like that."

"That's not the same thing at all," Mateo argued. "Where's the rush?"

"You plan to marry Lainey, right?"

"Damn straight."

"You got kids in mind?" Brax asked.

"Damn straight."

"I just can't help thinking that if I went through an injury like Jase did, and I had two kids with one on the way, I might be thinking of a change. That's all," Brax said as he continued to drive.

"One on the way?"

"Yep. Hadn't you heard?"

"Nope."

"Anyway, I think I could give up the rush for something a little more cerebral. Something a little safer, like working for a security firm."

"Shit. When you put it that way, I get it," Mateo said. He pointed to a mailbox up ahead. "There's the turn."

Brax turned in and they started down a long dirt road. They finally pulled up to a rickety old shack that looked like it had been built before the Civil War.

They parked in front of the house, then Brax knocked on the door. No one answered. Mateo went and peeked through one of the grimy windows, then shook his head.

"Let's look around back," Mateo suggested.

Brax nodded.

When they got to the back, they found Roy Jeckel, who looked nothing like the buttoned-up executive that they had seen in his picture. Instead, they found a relaxed man in old jeans and a flannel shirt, sitting on an upside-down milk crate. He was cutting up fish bait, and looked happy as could be.

"Mr. Jeckel?"

"I might be," he said when he looked up. "Depends on who you are."

"I'm Chief Petty Officer Braxton Walker, and this is Chief Petty Officer Mateo Aranda. We're here to ask you a few questions about Jenny Rivers."

Roy squinted up at them. "Were you two part of the team who rescued her?"

Brax nodded.

"You did good. I never met Jenny, but sometimes she'd be on a conference call with me and some others. Liked her. She had a sparkle. I will tell you that you've come to the wrong man if you want to know anything that came down regarding her. I don't know shit." The old man shook his head. "It was above my pay grade, but I was expected to spin things to make the company look good. You tell me, how in the hell was I supposed to spin a steaming pile of dogshit into gold?"

"Seems like it was an impossible task to me," Mateo said.

"Damned right it was. In my opinion, Ronald fucked up."

"Who's Ronald?" Brax asked.

"He's the Chairman of the Board. Was the CEO last

year. He got up off the milk box and picked up his fishing rod.

"How did Ronald fuck up?" Brax tried to keep Roy on topic.

"He should have paid the ransom. I know for a fact we had Kidnap and Ransom insurance. That's how we paid for a team to go in and rescue her. Why Ronald didn't just pay the ransom is beyond me. The company line was that we weren't sure who to pay the ransom to, and that's why it was withheld. You saw how well that went down with the media. Nobody bought that shit. If you want to know the truth, I think he withheld the money on purpose. Can't prove it. But two of us got multi-million-dollar retirement packages within two weeks of one another. VP of Security and me."

Brax looked over at Mateo, who nodded at him.

"I have just one more question. Do you know a guy by the name of Edgar Travis?"

"Never heard of him. Who is he?"

"Somebody Jenny worked with in London."

Roy threw back his head and laughed. "Now isn't that interesting."

"What?" Brax asked.

"Not many people know, but Ronald likes to fish even more than I do, only thing is, he does it in the company pond. I heard a rumor that he'd caught something in London."

"A woman named Fiona?" Mateo asked.

"Nope, he's not interested in women. But an Edgar might just be up his alley."

"We hear Edgar was embezzling money in London."

Roy grinned. "Even better. Ronald would have that over him, and he'd be able to keep him on a short leash forever. Ronald is ruthless. He would kill his own mother to come out on top, and he'd enjoy it. He'd love the idea of having something hanging over Edgar's head so he'd be at his mercy."

Roy baited his hook. "Still don't understand how this might have anything to do with Jenny, unless she was in on the embezzling or she was going to blow the whistle."

"It's complicated," Brax said. "Thank you so much for all of your help. You've been great."

"If you need me to testify against Ronald, I'd be more than happy to." He ticked off on his fingers. "I'm an only child. Never been married. No kids. I don't need the millions I got. Sticking it to Ronald is a lot more satisfying than the money."

Brax held out his hand. "It was really great to meet you."

Roy shook his hand.

When they got back to the car, Mateo laughed as Brax looked around in the cab of his truck to find a rag to wipe fish guts off his hand before he touched the steering wheel.

"You sure don't act like a SEAL," Mateo laughed.

"Shut it. I just detailed my car."

Mateo was still laughing as they were driving down the dirt road.

24

"I called Gideon and let him know we were done questioning Jeckel and we had info. He said that he had some, too. When I mentioned we were at Lake Anna, he laughed. Apparently, Kane has a lake house around here, so we're supposed to sit tight and wait for them."

"We passed a barbeque place on our drive in. Wanna go try it out while we wait for them?" Mateo asked.

"You know that all you're going to do is bitch about how the meat is cooked," Brax protested.

"That's half the fun."

"Fine," Brax acquiesced. He drove them back to the restaurant and they waited for a call from Gideon. Brax laughed when Mateo complained about how the meat was overcooked, but that was par for the course.

After an hour, they got a call from Gideon saying he and Kane were close. Gideon gave them the address to Kane's house.

"Let's roll."

When they pulled up to Kane's house, they were both still laughing when they got out of Brax's truck.

"What's so funny?" Kane asked as he got out of his vehicle at the same time.

"The last guy we visited here on the lake had a shack that looked like it was going to fall over in a stiff wind, and then we see this. The dichotomy is funny, is all," Mateo grinned.

"So which one do you like better?" Kane asked.

"I've got to see the inside," Mateo said.

"Did you find anything out?" Brax asked as they walked up the stairs to the front door.

"Yeah. We did," Gideon answered. "I was still working on something for the Lieutenant, so it was great that Kane could help."

Brax thought about Jada. He knew she could have helped as well, but he appreciated her taking Jenny's mind off everything.

When they got inside the house, the first thing Brax noticed was the big windows along the back that encompassed a view of Lake Anna. It was gorgeous. Kane sure had made it before he'd entered the service. Hell, so had Gideon.

"Can I get you anything to drink?" Kane asked.

"Water for me," Brax said. "I just had a beer at the barbeque place down the road."

"Same," Mateo said.

Kane got everybody what they wanted, then they followed him into a room that looked like a command center, what with all the high-end electronics.

"Here's what we found out," Kane said as he hitched

his hip against the corner of his desk, as the others took different seats around the room. "Soon after Jenny was transferred to Bangladesh, Edgar was transferred to the States. He was no longer working in finance, instead the CEO made up a bullshit job for him. Whoever heard of the Liaison of International Sub-Markets? When I dug deeper, all I could find was a two-sentence job description that showed he was reporting directly to the CEO. Seemed pretty fishy, so I dug deeper."

Brax glanced over at Mateo and saw his friend was struggling not to smile.

"Meanwhile," Gideon started. "I took on the task of finding out why New Era Cyber Tech sent in the team to rescue Jenny, but didn't pay the ransom. Turns out that anything like this falls under the purview of the VP of Security. Jeff Reynolds is his name, and as soon as Jenny was taken, he contacted the Kidnap and Ransom company that they had on tap, and they sent in a team to rescue her. It was by the book."

Brax nodded. Made sense. "Then what happened after they were killed?"

"Her ransom should have been paid," Gideon answered. "Now the Security guy, Jeff, doesn't have control of the company purse strings, so he had to go up the food chain. It went to the CEO. So, we immediately saw the connection between Edgar and the ransom. Anyway, Ronald told the VP of Security to hold off on paying the ransom."

"How'd you find that out?" Brax asked.

"The VP of Security got a multi-million dollar retirement a week after Jenny returned to the States. It was obviously a payoff. Last place we were able to track him was to Praslin Island in the Seychelle Island chain. He bought a yacht and has disappeared. There are over a hundred islands for him to go to, so we're not going to find him." Gideon was clearly annoyed.

"Then how do you know for sure it was a payoff?" Brax asked.

"We know that it was Ronald Lynch that was responsible because we found encrypted emails going back and forth between Ronald and Jeffrey, where Ronald specifically told Jeffrey that he was going to take over the ransom negotiation."

"Are you shitting me? How'd you find those? Seems to me a Security guy would have known enough to get rid of that kind of electronic trail," Brax said.

"That's not Jeff's area of expertise. All the cyber-security is handled by the IT department. My guess is, he had no idea about all of the company back-ups on email, especially the CEO's."

"Sounds like a shitty security guy," Brax said disgustedly.

"Yeah," Kane grinned. "Made my life easy. But I still haven't found out why the CEO would want to transfer an embezzler to the States as his flunky in a made-up job. It makes no sense. I'm still looking into that. I'm pulling both of their financials now."

"I think we can answer that." Mateo smirked.

Kane looked at him sharply and Gideon gave both of his men curious looks. "What do you mean?" Kane asked.

"Our meeting with Jeckel was quite enlightening,"

Brax answered. "Turns out, according to Jeckel, Ronald likes to fish off the company pier, and he likes men."

"Aw shit. Is this about sex?" Kane grumbled.

"Don't feel bad. Money is almost always the answer, but sex is usually the runner-up," Gideon soothed Kane.

Kane sat down at his desk chair and took a pull off his beer, then pointed his finger at Brax. "So, what's your supposition?"

"Ronald wanted Jenny dead to protect his lover. He didn't want anybody finding out about his embezzlement."

"That doesn't make any sense," Gideon protested. "Why kill her a year and a half after she supposedly found out about it? Why not sooner?"

"A crime of opportunity?" Mateo contributed.

"Why do it at all if she hadn't come forward before that point?" Gideon persisted.

"Could be that when her name popped up during the Bangladesh kidnapping, Edgar said something to Ronald. Then maybe Ronald gets upset and takes the opportunity to get rid of her. A crime of opportunity..." Kane shrugged.

Brax felt his blood begin to boil. The idea that someone could be so cavalier about Jenny's life made him want to kill someone.

"If that's the case," Gideon said slowly, "then does Ronald know about Fiona catching on and going into hiding?"

Brax jumped up. "Enough of this shit. We need to question Edgar."

"We can't right now. He and Ronald are at a summit in Paris. They're not due back for four days," Kane said, shaking his head.

"Then we go—" Brax started.

"No, we take the respite and figure out a plan," Gideon said.

Brax opened his mouth to disagree.

"We're dealing with one of the top ten biggest corporations in the world. We will not get anywhere close to either man without a plan," Gideon said decisively.

Brax nodded. He wasn't happy, but Gideon was right.

JENNY HAD NEVER SEEN Brax wound so tightly. He was like a different man. Even in the truck in Bangladesh he had exuded calm, but the entire drive home from Gideon's house, he seemed ready to explode. As they went up the little walkway to his porch his energy was so high that she saw him force himself to take little steps to match hers.

Her palms grew even clammier than they had been in the truck. What had she done wrong?

After he opened the door for her to walk through, Faith was there, excited to see them home. She bent down to give her love, but Brax just stalked past his dog.

What in the ever-loving hell?

"Fine, be mad at me, but don't take it out on Faith,"

Jenny said as Brax threw his truck keys in the fruit bowl.

Brax whirled around. "What are you talking about?"

Jenny pointed to where Faith was standing at his knee, waiting to be petted. "Faith. I'm talking about Faith. Don't take out your bad mood on her. I'm an adult. I can take you being mad at me, but it just confuses her when she has done nothing wrong, so stop it."

Brax crouched down and began scratching Faith behind her ears. "What are you talking about, me being mad at you? I'm not mad at you. As a matter of fact, this is the first time in hours that I feel like I can breathe."

Faith ran back to Jenny, and she patted her head.

Jenny looked at Brax and realized that behind his hard expression, there was pain. She gave Faith one last pat, then went over to Brax and ran her hands up his chest. "Tell me about it," she murmured.

"We figured out who wants you dead." His voice was strangled. It was as if the words came through a rusty pipe.

"Okay." Jenny waited for the other shoe to drop.

"Didn't you hear me?"

"Honey, that's a good thing, isn't it?"

He dropped his forehead to hers and took a deep breath. "Yes," he whispered. "Yes, it is."

She waited.

"You don't understand. I find a bad guy. I take him out. End of story. This is a hell of a lot more complicated than that. We're pretty sure that Ronald

Lynch is involved, and that's what makes it so complicated."

Jenny frowned. "The CEO?"

"That's the guy."

"Why would he want me dead? I'm a tiny little fish in the Cyber Tech ocean."

"I need a drink. What about you?" Brax asked.

"Sure, I'll get it," she offered.

"You go sit down on the couch. What would you like?"

"A little bit of that bourbon. But if it is really bad, maybe a little bit more than a little bit." Jenny went and sat down on the couch. Soon Brax came out with two glasses, one was twice as much as the other.

"Here you go." Jenny eyed her glass. It was far more than a little bit. It did not bode well.

"There better be snuggling to go along with the bourbon," she warned.

Brax sat down next to her and pulled her into his arms.

"Did you know that after you went to Bangladesh that Edgar Travers got transferred to the US?"

"Yeah. I heard it through the grapevine. To begin with, I thought they had found out about his embezzlement and that he was going to be arrested, but instead he was promoted. I told Fiona to continue to lie low." She took a small sip of her bourbon and watched Brax take a larger sip. "By the way, I called and left her a voicemail this afternoon. I did that when it was morning, her time. I should have done it sooner. I called Tina, and she was really mad that I hadn't been in touch."

Brax put down his drink, then plucked hers out of her hand. "Of course she was upset. How could you have anything but fantastic friends? I'm sure she loves you."

It was hard to keep eye contact with him when he was staring at her so intently, but she did. "That's what she said."

Brax cupped her jaw. "Of course she did. You're easy to love."

It felt like a balloon was welling up inside of her. It had started to expand when she'd talked to Tina, and now it was expanding so much she thought she might explode.

"You believe me, don't you?" Brax's voice was tender.

She bit the inside of her lip. "I think so."

"Then we'll work on that, because I do."

25

Jenny couldn't take it in.

It was hard to breathe, but dammit she was going to.

She took a deep breath.

She wanted to cry, but she wasn't going to.

"Got nothing to say?" Brax teased.

"You're worth loving, too," she whispered.

He hugged her hard and laughed. "We're getting there."

She needed to change the subject. "Why were you so mad when you came home today?"

"Because Edgar is in Paris and I can't get my hands on him."

"So, it's Edgar who's after me? But how does he know that Fiona told me anything?"

"He's probably just guessing. He knew you and Fiona were friends, right?"

Jenny nodded.

"From what you told me during our phone calls,

there weren't a lot of women who worked in the London office, so wouldn't it make sense that Edgar would assume you and Fiona would be friends?"

"I guess so. Fiona and I would go to lunch all the time, and sometimes Angela Polk would go with us."

"Who's Angela Polk?"

"She was the other executive assistant temp. We were the only three women on that floor."

"Were you good friends with her, too?"

"Not really, she was a loner. Most of the time she brought her lunch to work, but we'd always ask her to go with us."

"Of course you did," Brax said as he settled her on his lap.

"Do you think Edgar pushed me?"

"Probably not. My guess is he hired someone."

"And you're not mad at me? You were mad because you wanted to get your hands on Edgar?"

Brax chuckled as he pulled Jenny closer. "If I'm mad at you, I'll tell you. I don't like it when people are two-faced. Can't stand it. My mom was like that. She acted like everything was just fine, then ended up ripping the rug out from under our entire family. I promise, if there's a problem going on between the two of us, I'll let you know."

Jenny looked at Brax and tried to take his emotional temperature. He didn't seem upset anymore. Maybe, since he brought up his mom, he wanted to talk about her.

"What happened with your mom?" Jenny asked quietly.

"When I was eleven years old, CiCi was seven and her cancer came back for the third time. She was going into the hospital for another round of treatment." Brax cleared his throat. He reached for his glass, then his hand changed directions and came back to settle on her waist. He looked up at her and gave a crooked grin.

"I was a mama's boy. CiCi was daddy's little girl. Mom called me her little man." He took a deep breath and sighed. "When I look back on it as an adult, I can see how fucked-up that was. She told me things that she shouldn't have. She and dad didn't argue often, but when they did, she'd come to me and complain about him. She'd want me to take her side. That was such a party foul. You know?"

Jenny winced, trying to wrap her head around what he was saying. It was so different from the way she grew up. But yeah, she could see how a parent putting a kid in the role of an adult would be all kinds of wrong.

"What happened when you were eleven?"

"Mom and Dad were actually screaming and yelling at one another. That had never happened before. I heard everything. Mom planned to leave... Forever. Just up and leave while CiCi was in the hospital needing another round of chemotherapy. There CiCi was, with no hair, hurting like hell, and mom was going to take a runner. I couldn't believe it."

Jenny's eyes were wide as she took in what Brax was telling her.

"What was worse is, she came into my room and tried to justify it to me. Tried to get me on her side."

Still trying to make sense of what Brax was saying, Jenny asked, "why was she leaving?"

"She wanted to follow her dreams to live in the city and go to work at a magazine." Disgust dripped from his lips, like cold water from the tips of icicles.

"And did she? Did she leave?"

"After that day, I never saw her again. She called a couple of times, but I always hung up on her."

"At least my mom didn't leave on purpose," Jenny whispered.

"What?"

"Never mind," Jenny mumbled, looking down at the front of his shirt.

"No, you said your mom didn't leave on purpose. What happened to your mom?" Brax asked gently.

"She died from the flu. Dad didn't take her to the hospital, and she died. She left me all alone with Dad."

He pulled her tighter and put a knuckle under her chin, pushing up so he could see her face. "What are you saying, baby? What happened? How old were you?"

"I was a freshman. Fourteen. It was just me and him in the house."

Jenny glanced away from his intense gaze.

"He hurt you?" He asked the question gently, but she could hear the rage, pain and fear behind his words. She looked back at him, wanting to soothe him.

"Not real bad. Just punches and kicks and slaps and things. Same as always. It was worse since Mom wasn't there, 'cause he only had one target. I went to a couple of group counseling sessions in college. It could have been a lot, lot worse. I was lucky. Plus, I was fast, so I could get away from him easier than Mom ever could."

"Did you ever call anyone?"

"It never worked for Mom, why would it work for me?" Jenny shrugged.

Brax moved his hand and started to massage the nape of her neck, it felt heavenly.

"How'd you get away?" Brax eventually asked, continuing the massage.

"He dropped dead in the garage one night. Doctor said it was a heart attack."

"How old were you?" He whispered the question.

"Sixteen and a half. The sheriff and the doctor let me stay in the house."

"Honey, that doesn't make any sense. No social worker?"

"Neither of them was from our town. I made up an aunt who took care of me. They handled a lot of the little towns in our county, so they didn't know or much care. As long as their problem was solved, they were happy. All I had to do was finish out school and keep up my grades."

"Jesus."

Jenny pushed against his hand, silently asking for a deeper touch. When she got it, she continued her story. "As soon as I could, I started applying for scholarships, grants and anything else I could think of to get out of Wyoming. I got accepted to the University of Colorado in Aurora, outside of Denver. I was eighteen, so I got a real estate agent to help me sell the house for extra money, and the rest is history." She gave a half-hearted grin.

He moved her so that her legs bracketed his. She rested against his chest, and he could look her in the eye. "You are amazing."

"Hardly."

"Hand to God, you amaze me, Jenny Rivers."

She cupped his cheeks and stared into his eyes, soaking up his words.

Oh my God. He's telling me the truth. His truth.

"It's only fair to tell you, you amaze me, Braxton Walker," she whispered. "And do you know what else?"

His solemn look crept into a smile. "No, what?"

"You make me crazy, too."

"I do?" His hands slipped under the back of her thin sweater, and she shivered.

"Oh yeah. Let's see if I can make you crazy." She let go of his cheeks and wiggled so that she could reach the bottom of his long-sleeve t-shirt.

She could.

Brax made it very easy for her to pull it over his head, and when she was done, she threw it over her shoulder.

Woof.

"Someone else wants to get in on the action," Jenny giggled.

Brax frowned. "This is adult playtime, so it's only you and me." Somehow, by magic, he was able to stand up from the couch with her still in his arms.

"How'd you do that?"

"Lower and upper body strength." With one hand

under her ass, he hitched her up higher and walked them into his bedroom. He paused after they made it over the threshold. "Close the door, baby."

Jenny did.

Brax walked them to the bed and lowered her to the mattress like precious cargo.

EVERY SINGLE TIME he thought he'd plumbed the depths of Jenny Rivers, he found out he was wrong. The woman had gone through more, survived more, and come up fighting. She had the soul of a warrior. And here she was in his bed, her arms reaching up for him.

Brax knew she loved him. She showed it in so many ways, and her heartfelt speech the first time they'd made love was definitely a declaration of love, but his woman was scared to death of loving someone and being let down. That was fine by him. He could live the rest of his life never hearing the words, as long as he had Jenny in his arms, in his bed, in his life.

He watched as she slowly undulated on his silver sheets.

"Why are you standing there? I thought we were going to play?"

"I'm just taking my time, figuring out my first move," Brax answered.

"Like chess?"

"Exactly like chess," he agreed. "Looking over the board, I'd say I'm at a disadvantage. You have too many clothes on."

Her smile was pure seduction. "So do something about it."

He leaned down and took off her sneakers and socks, then massaged her small feet. He heard her soft moan. He pushed his thumbs into her arches.

"That feels good."

"It's supposed to."

He tried to push up farther, up to her calves, but was stopped by the tight denim. The jeans had to go. He put a knee on the bed and made quick work of the fastenings and stripped her out of her panties and jeans. He looked up and saw her face was still suffused with passion. Good, because he wanted her completely naked.

"Sit up," he commanded.

"Don't want to."

He pulled at her arms, and she mewed in mock protest. He divested her of her sweater and bra, before slowly releasing her back to the sheets.

"Now you're at a disadvantage," he said.

"That's not the way I see it," Jenny teased. "Seems to me, I've got your full attention." She was looking pointedly at his groin where the outline of his hard cock was visible under his jeans. Brax laughed.

"You always have my full attention." He said as he took off his belt, not wanting to mark her skin, then lay down on the bed beside her and took her into his arms, cupping her ass, just because he could.

"Why aren't you naked yet?" she asked.

"I want to take my time."

"Nooo," she wailed. "No taking time. I want you inside me now!"

Brax laughed again. "You're greedy, has anyone ever told you that?"

She reached up and brushed her fingers along his temple. "Before you, it's only been about chocolate."

"Are you telling me I rank as high as chocolate?"

"I don't know. Because. You're. Not. Inside. Me." She reared up and nipped at his chin.

And here he had been worrying about her after all of her revelations. Jenny was fire and spice, someone who could never be contained. But that didn't mean he wasn't going to spend his life doing everything he could to protect her.

She rubbed one hand up his chest, and one hand slid into his jeans. "I really think these need to go," she coaxed.

He jumped up from the bed and shucked out of his clothes. He leaned over her. Her legs were twisting around in the sheets, a sure sign of arousal, but he needed to make sure. He batted away her hand that was reaching for his cock and slid his hand between her thighs.

She was soft as butter. He pressed in two fingers.

"Yes," she cried. "Like that."

She shoved herself off the bed, so that only her feet and shoulders were holding herself up. Brax started a rhythm with his fingers. He felt for that spot that would render magic, then he found it. Jenny went tight as a bowstring.

She continued to cry out his name, as he took her

higher and higher. Sweat trickled down his back as he watched his lover climb her way up to ecstasy. She was radiant.

One more stroke of his fingers and she shattered. He shoved his free arm under her waist to lower her gently back down to earth, as he pulled out his fingers and licked them clean.

He didn't know how long it was going to take her to be ready for him, but he was content to wait.

Bullshit.

One green eye opened, as Jenny slowly spread her thighs wider. "That was only a Hershey's Kiss," she slurred. "Now I'm ready for some hot fudge."

Thank fuck.

Brax rolled over to the nightstand and grabbed a condom out of the drawer. His hands shook as he put it on. She must have noticed because she smiled with satisfaction.

Brax took a moment just to admire Jenny, the soft sheen that covered her skin, the slight dusting of freckles across her nose, the feminine pink that beckoned him, and those green eyes that radiated all the love in the world. His woman.

He entered her as slow as he could, savoring every second of their joining. Jenny wrapped her arms around his shoulders and he buried his face in her neck, breathing in her essence. He started moving. Her breathing quickened, and so did his. They savored this moment, then he turned for a kiss. But like all things between them, it soon turned into a wildfire.

The scorching flavor of all that was Jenny rocketed

through his system, taking him somewhere he had never been before. His body surged faster inside her as he tried to inhale her very essence. She twisted in his arms, she was so close. He was so close, too.

She was his and he was hers, and finally they shot into a universe that nobody but them had ever reached before. A place just for two hurt souls, made for one another.

26

Jenny didn't think she'd ever been so happy in her life, as she opened the door and bent down to pick up the package that the UPS driver had just left. She just wished that Brax could feel the same way. Apparently, Edgar and Mr. Lynch were staying longer in Paris, and that had Brax and some of the rest of the team acting like they had ants in their pants. Come to think of it, she was going to get in trouble for having picked up the package off the front porch while Brax was at work. But she couldn't help it, she was excited.

Clothes!

As she put the box down on the kitchen table, her cell phone rang.

"Damn, does Brax have cameras in this place?"

She scrambled to the bedroom and pulled her phone off her charger.

Fiona!

"Hey, Fiona! where in the hell have you been?" Jenny exclaimed.

"In Australia. I went there on a long holiday with a great guy. You'd really like him. Sorry I haven't been answering my phone, but that was part of the deal. He wouldn't answer his phone unless it was an emergency, and neither would I."

That made sense. "You really like this guy, huh?"

"Yeah. I think he could be the one. You know? I just hate lying about who I am."

"That's why I wanted to talk to you."

"Do you know something?" Fiona asked eagerly.

Jenny winced and sat down on the side of the bed. "Nothing good, I'm afraid."

"Has Edgar tracked down where I'm at?" Jenny hated the level of fear she heard in her friend's voice.

"No, nothing like that. I promise."

"That's good. Then what is it?"

"Edgar and the CEO of Cyber Tech are involved, and that's why the company wouldn't pay my ransom when I was kidnapped in Bangladesh."

"What? Kidnapped? What are you talking about?"

Jenny closed her eyes and tilted her head up to the ceiling. "You didn't hear? It made the national news here in the US. I guess I just assumed you'd heard about it."

"Jenny, tell me what happened," Fiona ordered.

"Cyber Tech wouldn't pay my ransom, basically leaving me to be killed by my kidnappers. Luckily, an American Navy SEAL team rescued me."

"Bloody hell, Jenny, that's horrible. How long were you held captive?"

"Three weeks. But that doesn't matter. What

matters is that the CEO wanted me dead, and we figure it's because Edgar told him something to make him believe I know about his embezzling. I'm still wrapping my head around somebody wanting to kill me. Then they tried again."

"Oh Jenny," Fiona whispered. "I am so sorry that I ever involved you in this."

Jenny could hear anguish in Fiona's voice.

"It's not your fault, you didn't know that it would get to this point."

"I always knew Edgar had it in him, I just didn't think it would be directed at you."

"What are you talking about?"

"He didn't just put money into an account in my name, he did it to the other temp, Angela."

"Why didn't you tell me?" Jenny was stunned.

"Three days before I left town, Angela died in a hit and run. I went to the police station. They told me that the driver actually sped up when she was in the crosswalk. They didn't have a lot of hope of finding the driver because the plates were muddy and the windows were tinted. It was just another black Ford near King's Cross. You know everybody drives those."

"So, Edgar killed her when she found out what he had done," Jenny murmured.

"She told me that she was going to call the States, and she'd told Edgar that. That's why she quit. Because she quit, before she was killed, and she was just a temp, nobody knew about her death. Nobody but me."

"Why in the hell did she ever tell him she was going to blow the whistle?" Jenny got up off the bed and walked to the living room, unable to stay still any longer.

"Your guess is as good as mine. You know I was already making plans to leave, but as soon as she told me that, that's when I slept on your couch. I can never thank you enough for that."

"It was only for three nights. I can't believe you were able to come up with a new identity that fast and move to Spain."

"Yeah, well, I grew up in a sink estate—"

"Sink estate?"

"Like your projects. Like a bad neighborhood. I still had some friends from way back. What I can't believe is that Edgar's after you. You need to run, too."

"No, I don't. Edgar has to be stopped."

"How can he be stopped if Mr. Lynch is on his side? He has more power than God."

"I think it is mostly Edgar who is doing everything. I don't think Mr. Lynch wants to lose everything he has by getting involved in this."

"But he didn't pay your ransom."

"That's not the same thing as trying to outright kill me," Jenny said slowly. *Maybe Edgar had something hanging over Mr. Lynch's head.*

"You said that there was another attempt on your life." Fiona interrupted Jenny's thoughts.

"Somebody pushed me into oncoming traffic."

Fiona snorted. "Sure sounds like Edgar's MO."

"You're right about that. Look, I need to get off the phone and tell my guy about all of this. He'll need all of this new information."

"Who's your guy?"

"He's one of the SEALs who rescued me. I'm living at his house for the time being."

Fiona barked out a laugh. "Is he hot?"

"Shit. Why do all my friends ask me that question?" Jenny demanded.

"Because it's important," Fiona laughed. "So, is he hot?"

"Yes, he is, and yes I've slept with him."

"Good for you. Okay, go tell your SEAL."

"Good-bye Fiona."

"Stay safe, Jenny."

JENNY CALLED BRAX, and he said he'd be home in less than an hour. She needed something to take her mind off her conversation with Fiona so she went to the kitchen and opened her package. She mentally rubbed her hands together as she pulled out item after item. She couldn't believe how much she'd let Jada and Leila talk her into spending, but as she rubbed her fingers along the lush fabrics and felt the smooth linings of the suit jacket, she grinned like a fool.

She was in the second bedroom when the doorbell rang. After hearing everything that Fiona had to say, she didn't just run to the door, she approached it with caution.

Woof.
Woof.
Woof.

"Whoever's behind the door is a friend, huh Faith?"

Jenny looked through the peephole, grinned, unlocked the door, and opened it wide.

"Oh my God, the clothes came," Jada said as she looked Jenny up and down. She shut the door behind her and waved Jenny to the middle of the living room. "Turn around."

Jenny did a circle.

"That dress is gorgeous on you. I just wish it was summer already."

Jenny looked down at the yellow sundress. "So do I. I can't believe I let you talk me into buying this. I don't need it right now."

"It was fifty percent off the clearance price. It fits you like a dream. Of course you had to get it. It offset the costs of the other clothes."

Jenny shook her head. "Jada, that's not how math works."

"Sure, it is. When you look at it that way, most of my shoes only cost about forty dollars a pair."

Jenny laughed at Jada. Just laughed at her. She'd seen her rebuilt shoe closet. She had designer shoes that she'd seen worn by models in Vogue magazine.

"You're so full of shit."

"Stick with me, and learn the ways of the world." Jada grinned. "Now go try on something else before we're surrounded by male aggression."

Jenny sobered. "It's not going to be good."

"I didn't think so, otherwise Gideon wouldn't have asked me to clear my calendar," Jada said as she trailed Jenny into the bedroom.

Jenny looked over her shoulder. "He doesn't even know what I'm going to say."

"Those boys will have a hair trigger until Edgar is put away. That's just the way they roll."

"Do you want to know?" Jenny asked.

"Nah, tell us all together. I want to see clothes. Hustle up."

JENNY WAS SITTING in one of Brax's fluffy chairs, Gideon and Jada were sitting across from her on the couch, and Brax was sitting beside her on the arm of the chair with his hand on her shoulder. She'd just told them about her conversation with Fiona.

"Let's get her on the phone so I can talk to her," Gideon said.

"What's the point?" Jenny asked with a frown.

"We want to track down those accounts that are in her name and track them back to Edgar," Jada said soothingly.

"I can't believe she kept you in the dark about Angela being killed. That left you with a big target on your back, without you knowing about it. She's not a good friend." Brax squeezed her shoulder tighter.

"Neither of us knew that Edgar would think that I had anything to do with her or Angela," Jenny protested.

"Bullshit," Brax said. "It was obvious."

Jenny cringed. Brax was right, and she really didn't want to admit it to herself. She really liked Fiona.

"Look, we need to talk to Fiona so we can track down those accounts. We need some evidence against this bastard when we confront him," Gideon said.

Brax's head shot up and he glared at his friend. "We don't need shit. Just give me two minutes alone with him, and I'll find out everything we need to know. Then I want another two minutes alone with that fucking CEO."

"Brax." Gideon's voice was one that Jenny hadn't heard before. It must have been his commander voice. "We're not out in the field. We're here in the US dealing with two prominent men in a Fortune 100 corporation. We've got to have our ducks in a row."

"One left Jenny hanging in the wind in Bangladesh on a maybe chance that she might know something about his lover, and the other one killed one woman in England and attempted to kill Jenny right here in Virginia."

"Yeah, but we have no proof."

"And I just said I can—"

Jenny put her hand on Brax's thigh and gently squeezed. He looked down at her and she mouthed the word, *please*.

Brax nodded.

"Okay. But we better have a plan of action by the time they get home from Paris," Brax growled.

27

"I don't need a damn babysitter," Jenny said, her hands on her hips. God, she looked good. This was the first time he'd seen her hair done, make-up on, dressed in a suit and heels. Right now, he'd give her about anything she'd ask for, except when it came to her safety.

"Jenny, you know Edgar and Ronald flew in on Cyber Tech's jet early this morning. Gideon and Jada have found out all the information they needed to prove that Edgar funneled money out of Fiona and Angela's shell corporations and put them into accounts that belong to him. They've got a tidy little report that they can give to authorities, but we want more. We want confessions, so we're going to go visit Edgar, and when we do, I want you at Gideon's house. That's the safest place for you to be."

"Brax, I have an interview this afternoon. Mr. Grant could only fit me in at four-thirty."

"I'm sorry, Honey. You're going to have to cancel it."

"I don't understand why you've got your undies in a bunch. You've just said that you know where Edgar and Mr. Lynch are going to be. I should be safe. Also, they shouldn't know I'm at your house."

"Did you send a resume with Cyber Tech as one of your jobs?" Brax asked.

Jenny nodded.

"Don't you think the hiring manager called for references?"

Jenny tapped her foot. "No, I don't. They only do that after they interview you and are interested in hiring you. So, no, big guy, Cyber Tech won't know I'm there. Now you see why I don't need to go to Gideon and Jada's house."

Brax rubbed the back of his neck. "Jenny," he said softly. "Can you do it for me? I just don't feel good about things. I want you safe."

She stopped tapping her toe and took her hands off her hip. Her expression softened. "Why didn't you say it that way from the start? I'll put off interviewing until after this is over with."

Brax stepped forward, and she met him in the middle. "I don't deserve you," he whispered into her sweet-smelling hair.

"You've got that the wrong way around," she whispered into his chest.

AT THE LAST MINUTE, Gideon was pulled back to Little Creek by Kostya to clear up a situation, and that put their operation timeline on hold. Brax felt even better about things. Confronting Edgar in the middle of the night was sure to have him shitting his pants. Especially how they intended to do it.

Edgar Travers lived in a plush condominium in downtown Richmond. Mateo would bypass the building's security and put the camera feeds from Edgar's floor on a repeating loop for one hour. Within that time, Gideon, Brax and Mateo would go up the delivery elevator with a laundry cart that contained their gear. Confronting Edgar with night-vision goggles, bulletproof vests, and assault rifles should capture his attention as they discussed his involvement with the death of Angela Polk.

They intended to get his confession on video.

Easy.

Or maybe not.

As soon as they entered the condo, the hair on the back of Brax's neck stood on end. Something was not right. He gave the signal to spread out and proceed with caution. It wasn't until they got to the last room, the primary bedroom, that he found out why. Edgar was on his bed, his sleeve rolled up, a rubber tourniquet tied around his upper arm, and a hypodermic needle hanging out of his vein. There was foam around his blue lips, and his dead eyes were partially open.

All three of them took off their night vision goggles and Brax turned on the bedroom light. They touched nothing.

Beside the corpse was a spoon, a baggie of what had to be heroin, and a lighter. A cheap lighter.

Brax saw the pack of Parliament cigarettes on Edgar's dresser. There was a lighter beside it that looked gold-plated. "Take a look at this." He nodded at the expensive lighter.

"Someone sure did a shitty job of setting up this overdose." Gideon said in disgust.

"Ronald?" Mateo asked. "But why would he? Why not just cut him loose? People dump their boyfriends or girlfriends all the time," Mateo asked.

"Because now Ronald is an accessory after the fact of the embezzling, and I'm sure that Edgar has pointed this out," Brax said slowly. "Or better yet, he's an accessory after the fact of Angela's murder."

"Yep, I'm sure he would have pointed that out," Gideon agreed. "Now Ronald wants all the players off the board."

"How do we get to Ronald?" Mateo asked.

"We're sure as hell not going to be all nice and get a paper trail. Now I get to get him in a room alone, and this time I want four minutes." Brax caught a glimpse of his face in the mirror above the dresser. He looked deadly.

JENNY SMILED when she saw her friend's number come up on the screen. "Hi, Tina. Did you like the picture I sent you of the interview look?"

"Uhmm, I didn't see it," Tina said.

"You didn't?"

"Uhmm, no."

Jenny frowned. "Are you okay?"

Jada looked up from where she was watching a reality TV show, and Jenny shrugged.

"Look, Jenny, I really wanted to come and visit you. Remember when I said that?"

"Sure. I can't wait to see you." Jenny smiled. "But I think I should come out to you. Brax snowboards. So, it will be perfect for us to come out and hit the slopes. There's just a couple of little things that need to be sorted—"

"Stop! Just stop!"

"Tina, honey, what's wrong?"

"I'm sorry. Let me start again. I came to visit you. I wanted to surprise you. I'm near the Norfolk airport, but my rental car broke down and my phone's about to die."

"Honey, I'm having trouble understanding you. Are you safe?"

Tina sobbed.

"I'm going to call the police," Jenny said firmly.

"No! You can't. I just need you to come and get me. I need to see you. Please. Can you come and get me?"

"Do you know where you are?"

"When I drove in it said Norfolk Industrial Park. I'm in a parking lot somewhere on Village Road. Can you please come and get me? I'm in a white Toyota Corolla."

"Okay honey. Are you under a light?"

"Yes. And I have mace. Just come and get me. Okay?"

Jenny checked her phone and from James Lake, she

calculated it would take about fifteen minutes to get there. "I should be there in less than twenty minutes. Okay?"

"Okay. I'm so sorry, Jenny. So sorry."

"What for? This is what friends are for."

Jenny disconnected and turned to Jada. "Did you hear?"

"Yep, sounds like we're going to pick up your friend. She sounds pretty shaky, are you sure we shouldn't call the police?"

"I think that would spook her even more at this point. Let's just go get her and bring her back here." Then the idea of seeing her friend that she hadn't seen in over three years hit her brain and Jenny grinned. "Jada, you're going to love her."

"I'll text Gideon."

"I'll text Brax."

WHAT THE FUCK? He re-read his text from Jenny. "Gideon, how far away are we from your house?" Brax demanded to know.

"Seventy miles."

"And to the airport?" Brax asked.

"About the same."

Brax dialed Jenny. "Go back to the house. It's a setup."

"What are you talking about?" Jenny sounded perplexed.

"It's a setup." Brax repeated himself.

"My best friend would not be setting me up." He could hear the exasperation in her voice.

Brax rubbed the back of his neck. The same hairs that had been standing up when they'd entered Edgar's condo were standing on end now. He put his phone on speaker so Mateo and Gideon could hear.

"Jenny, your best friend just called you and said that she flew in from Colorado, unannounced, and that her car is broken down near some warehouses, and she wants you to come and pick her up. Is that right?"

"Yes."

"Why haven't you called the police?"

"That would just scare her more. She's a nervous traveler, anyway. Jada's with me."

"Jada, tell me you're not falling for this shit," Gideon groaned.

"Maybe," his fiancée strung out the word.

"Both of you go back home and wait for us," Gideon ordered.

"She's scared. I'm picking up my friend." Jenny was beginning to get mad, Brax could tell.

"Call the police. Have them arrive when you do."

There was a long pause, then finally, Jenny responded. "Okay, I can do that."

"Jada, you know where the gun is in the Range Rover. Take it with you."

"Gotcha."

28

"She hung up the phone!" Brax hit his fist against the passenger door of Gideon's Ford 450. "What the fuck?"

Mateo chuckled from the backseat. "Call her back."

"She better answer," Brax said as he dialed.

She picked up immediately. "Now what do you want to tell me? Have you bought stock in bubble wrap?"

"This is serious, Jenny."

"I've got the gun. I called the police, they're on their way. We're good. In less than five minutes I'm going to be hugging Tina. Now mellow."

Brax blew out a deep breath and smiled. Good. This wasn't going to go like all the other clusterfucks that had gone on with every other woman of Omega Sky.

"I'm going to be doing more than just hugging you in an hour and twenty minutes," he crooned.

"I can't decide if I'll agree to that. On one hand,

you've been a domineering jackass, on the other hand, you sure do care about me."

"Don't hang up until you get back to Gideon's, okay? No matter what, you don't hang up, and you don't let go of this phone. I want to hear everything. Do you understand me?"

"Aye-aye."

He heard Jenny talking to Jada. "Is Gideon like this?"

"They all are," Jada answered her back.

"She didn't happen to say which corner, did she?" Jada asked in a louder voice.

"No," Jenny answered. "Just on Village Road."

"Shit. We're going to have to drive just a little bit. Holler if you see her."

"Why are all the cars in these parking lots either white or gray?" Jenny asked.

Brax felt like ants were crawling in his ears.

Where were the police?

"How many cars do you see?" Gideon asked.

"About six or seven in each parking lot," Jada answered. "Haven't seen any people yet. Not every parking lot has lights."

"Hey, I think I see the car," Jenny said. "Across the street."

Where are the police, for fuck's sake?

"Jenny, wait for the police," Brax shouted.

"We're fine, Brax. No bogeymen in sight. I've got to go to her. She's scared to death. Jada, here's the gun. I've got my phone. I'll go knock on the window," Jenny said.

"She knows me, two of us showing up will scare her with the state she was in."

Then Brax heard Jenny get out of the Range Rover.

JENNY WISHED she was wearing something warmer than a suit jacket, skirt, and shoes more comfortable than high heels. She put her hands in her jacket pockets to warm them and continued walking the short distance over to the Toyota, smiling in anticipation. When she didn't see Tina's head in the driver's window she slowed down.

"Tina?" she called out.

The driver's window started rolling down and she smiled again, rushing forward. "Girl, how are you?"

Up popped a clown with a gun. She stuttered to a halt.

Lik a giant jack in the box.

"Keep coming," the clown crooned.

Jenny couldn't. Her feet were glued to the cement.

"I said keep coming. You want to see your friend alive again, don't you?" Jenny nodded.

It was a set-up. Brax was right.

"Cops are coming, you won't get away with this," she blurted out.

"Jenny, how's Tina?" Jada shouted from the Range Rover.

"Say, 'fine.'"

"Fine," Jenny did her best to shout back.

"Now get in the car and we're going to go on a little drive."

Jenny stood up straight. "No. You're going to end up killing me anyway, so no."

"You're right. But you can save the life of that pretty woman over there, if you get in the car with me and we go." He moved the gun and aimed at Jada.

Jenny rushed around to the passenger seat.

"Jenny, what are you doing?" Jada called out.

"Tina just wants to tell me something really quick. We'll be over there in just a minute."

"Good girl," the clown rumbled as Jenny opened the passenger door and got in. It smelled like cigarettes.

"You can't smoke in a rental car," she told him.

Where had that come from?

He laughed. "Yeah, that's the sin I'm worried about."

Then he shot twice at the Range Rover before tearing out of the parking lot.

Jenny sat there in shock, then lunged at him. "You promised you wouldn't kill her!"

He hauled back and hit her hard with the butt of his gun. "I didn't, you stupid bitch. I shot out her tires."

Jenny looked over her shoulder and saw Jada running into the street. She took a shooter's stance and fired off a round. Nothing happened. Everything started to get fuzzy. Jenny felt tears rushing down her face.

No wait.

That was blood.

So fuzzy.

"Where are you—"

Nothing.

Everything went black.

"I don't ask for much out of life, do I?" a familiar voice said.

"Well, actually you do." It was the clown speaking. She recognized his voice.

Jenny coughed. The cigarette smell was making her nauseous. But at least she wasn't in a car anymore. Where was she?

"Each time I ask for something, you ask for more money, and I pay you, and you fuck up. This is not a good return on my investment."

"Yeah, well, I'm the only guy you know to take care of these kinds of problems, so you're stuck with my lousy ROI. I did get rid of that namby-pamby idiot you were fucking. Made it look like he was a druggie."

"So, you're one out of three. I do hope when she wakes up you can better your score."

"Or what? You're going to hire someone to take me out?" The clown laughed. More cigarette smoke blew her way, and Jenny rolled over and threw up. The vomit got all in her hair and on the side of her face. The only reason she cared was that the puke messed up her vision in the eye that wasn't swollen shut. Now she was basically blind.

"Put out that cigarette," the man who wasn't the clown yelled.

"Where's Tina? What did you do to Tina?" Jenny choked out the question.

The clown laughed. "Nothing. She's safe and sound in Colorado. Just had her husband knocked out for a couple of hours so she thought we had him. Told her to make that call or we'd kill him. Worked like a charm. They're probably canoodling by the fire right now, not giving one fucking thought about you."

Jenny blew out a long breath, so thankful that her friend was safe.

"Tell us what we want to know."

"Mr. Lynch?" Jenny asked.

"Yes."

"You're going to let him kill me, aren't you?"

"Yes. I'd like him to do it so it's painless. I told him to get a vial of narcotics so you would just fade away. But you'll only receive that kind of death if you cooperate."

She wanted to see his face. Here he was, a man who had everything, stooping down to murder. And for what?

"I'll tell you where Fiona is, if you tell me why you're doing this. I respected you. I don't understand, and before I die, I want to understand."

"Good girl, keep him talking," Brax whispered.

His hands were so sweaty, he was afraid he was going to drop his phone. He kept staring down at it, making sure the mute button was on. It was. Waiting for her to wake up took years off his life. He hadn't prayed this much since CiCi had been in the hospital, hell, he was probably praying more.

"Where are they?" Gideon asked.

Brax looked down at the tracking app. "They've stopped at a place on Westminster Avenue near Grandy Village."

"Give me the address, I'll plug it into the navigation system," Mateo said from the backseat.

Brax gave him the info, desperately waiting for someone to talk.

"Edgar was such a disappointment," Ronald said. "I should have had him prosecuted the minute I found out about the embezzlement, but by the time I did, I was in too deep. I'd already given him a promotion and brought him to the States. And Edgar was more than happy to point that out."

"He blackmailed you?"

"I was about to turn the tables on him, when Jeffrey here told me about the untimely death of Angela Polk. When I confronted Edgar, he admitted to her murder. I was fucked. A month later you were kidnapped. Finally, fortune was smiling down on me. Until Jeffrey screwed the pooch."

Brax looked over at Gideon. "Just the two of them."

"Sounds like," Gideon agreed.

"We've got this." Mateo stated with confidence.

"How long to get there?" Brax asked Mateo.

"Eleven more minutes, brother. We've had worse

timelines than this, and come out alive, we've got this." Mateo reached over from the back seat and squeezed Brax's shoulder.

Brax stared down at the phone in his hand and kept praying.

"How did Jeffrey screw up?" Jenny coughed. The blood that had been dripping down her face was starting to congeal. She still couldn't see.

"He sent in a rescue team before talking to me."

"I'm sorry, boss."

I'm going to hate clowns for the rest of my life. Let's just hope it's a long one.

"Yeah, I heard about that," Jenny said. "They all died."

"That was lucky." She could hear the glee in the CEO's voice. "But then they sent in the fucking SEALs to rescue you. What a mess."

Jenny flinched when she heard a crash and breaking glass. It was like he had thrown something against a wall.

"Then that fucker, Henry Roberts, had to blab to the Washington Post, and it made national news that I hadn't paid the ransom."

Jenny smelled cigarette smoke.

"Goddammit Jeff, I told you to go outside if you have to smoke!"

"Who cares, the house already reeks."

"I care. Put out the cigarette."

How much longer before Brax gets here?

"Now you know everything. My last two loose ends are you and your friend Fiona. Tell me where she is, and I'll let you die easy. If you don't tell me where she is, Jeff will start cutting off body parts."

"Jesus, boss. That's just sick."

"Shut up, you pussy. You already pushed her into traffic. What does it matter if you torture her? I told you I would pay you more for wet work. Instead of a yacht, you can buy an entire island."

Jenny felt her gorge rising. She was going to throw up again. She could taste the vomit coming up. Puke spilled out of her mouth.

"Hah. Look at her. She'll be pissing her pants next," Ronald crowed. "Tell us where Fiona is."

"I hurt too much. I can't think." It wasn't tough for Jenny to make her voice sound weak.

"Hell boss, all we need is her phone. We can do the same play with her, like we did with Jenny's friend Tina."

Oh God, don't let them look for my phone. It was tucked inside a pocket in her suit jacket.

"She doesn't have her purse. Fiona's in Europe, you ass. We're here in America. How's that supposed to work? I want this bitch dead tonight. We can't afford to be dragging her around the world with us, even on the company jet."

"Yeah," the clown muttered. "I guess you're right. Answer the question. Where is Fiona? I've got a syringe loaded up. You'll just float away. Take the easy way out, Jenny."

"No." She tried to sound strong.

"Ahhhh!" The pain of a knife slicing through the silk shell of her top and into her flesh burned like fire. Indescribable pain. Worse—she hadn't known it was coming.

29

"There!" Brax yelled. "Turn there!"

Gideon turned, but not fast enough. Brax knew in his head that he was doing the right thing, but it was killing him. Now was not the time for screeching tires. Gideon double parked a block down the street from the target house.

All three men jumped out of the car, grabbing their weapons. They ran down the street. They were in the bad part of town, and when they passed three young men sitting on a porch stoop, they turned their heads.

Brax was running slower than Gideon and Mateo because he still had the phone up to his ear. He heard Jenny gasping for breath.

"Now tell me where Fiona is," Ronald asked again.

"Portugal," Jenny said so softly that Brax could barely hear her.

"You're going to have to narrow that down some. You're also going to have to tell us the name she's currently using." Ronald sounded so reasonable it made Brax go ice cold. He could see Mateo scouting the perimeter of the east side of the house. Gideon had disappeared around the west side.

Jenny was continuing to breathe in short painful pants.

"Tick tock," Jeffrey said. "I don't like cutting you, but I will if you don't start talking. Hell, you heard the man, I'll get to buy an island. Hey boss, where should I cut next?"

"Her alias is Simonne LeGare. She lives in Braga."

"That's still not enough."

"I can't think of any more," Jenny wailed.

Gideon came back to the front of the house. He motioned Brax and Mateo toward him. They gathered around. "They have her in the basement. There are three windows, none of them large enough to get through. Decorative only. The only other egress is stairs leading up to the kitchen. They're not facing the stairs, Jenny is."

"And the windows?" Brax asked.

"They're up and to their left. There are racks with boxes in front of them. Shots will be difficult, but not impossible." Gideon answered.

"I want the stairs," Brax said.

Mateo and Gideon nodded.

"We'll be at the windows," Gideon said. "We'll hold fire until you make a move unless Jeff starts in on her again."

They all nodded.

Through it all, Brax had had his phone on speaker, the only sound had been Jenny's harsh breathing. They broke apart and went their separate ways.

Brax easily broke the lock on the back kitchen door and crept inside. The house was a shambles, it looked like it had been used as a meth house at one point. He spotted the door that led to the basement. It wasn't closed shut. He nudged it open just enough to squeeze past the opening and looked at the wooden stairs. Silently, he stepped on the outer edges of each stair as he crept down.

"Uhmm, I'm thinking. Honest. I'm thinking."

"How about where she works?" Ronald asked. "Do you know where she works?"

"Yes!" Jenny cried out excitedly. "It's for a graphic design company. It starts with a C."

"Jeffrey, cut her again."

Rage like he had never felt before, flowed through his body as Brax bent down so he could see past the overhang and look at the scene in front of him. Ronald had a gun hanging from his fingertips at his side, and Jeffrey was nudging up Jenny's skirt with the tip of his knife. Brax lifted his gun, took aim, and fired.

Jenny screamed.

Brax fired again as he heard two more shots.

Jenny continued to scream and scream and scream.

Jeffrey collapsed onto Jenny. Brax rushed to her, picked up Jeffrey's body, and flung it away.

"Brax, you came."

"Of course I did."

He crushed her to his chest, uncaring about the blood and vomit that covered her. He cupped her cheeks so he could look in her eyes. One eye was swollen shut, the other stuck shut with blood and vomit.

"Jenny, can you see me?"

"No. Can you wipe my face off?"

"How'd you know it was me?"

"Because you'll always come to my rescue."

EPILOGUE
THREE MONTHS LATER

"I NOW PRONOUNCE YOU, HUSBAND AND WIFE. YOU MAY kiss your bride."

Jenny watched as Gideon tenderly kissed Jada. She watched for just a moment, but then turned away, it was too private a moment. Their love was a beautiful thing, and Jenny was amazed and honored that Jada had asked her to be one of her bridesmaids.

When they were done, everybody started to clap and hoot and holler, and Jenny turned back to see Jada and Gideon's big grins.

"Let's get this party started," Jada yelled.

There was no subdued walk back down the aisle for Jada Marlow-Smith, nope, she practically ran with Gideon as they headed to the back of the church and a waiting limousine that would take them to the reception venue.

The rest of the bridal party was moving along behind, as they should be. Kostya escorted Lark down the aisle at a subdued pace, followed by Ryker and

Amy, then Linc and Leila, Jase and Bonnie, Mateo and Lainie, and finally her and Brax. They met up in the parking lot with the single members of Omega Sky and members of Night Storm and Jada's family, then everyone went to their cars to head over to the magical venue that had been chosen for the reception.

When they got to the reception, it was even more beautiful than the pictures Jada had shown the women. Brax went to go get them something to drink, and Jenny looked up at all the balloons that covered the ceiling.

"Isn't this amazing?" Bonnie asked her as she sidled up next to her.

Jenny gave Bonnie's tummy a sideways glance.

"Don't look at me like that. I'm not having twins again. I promised Jase. It's just that he's a big guy, and I'm having his big baby."

Jenny laughed. "How's everything going?"

"A lot better than I could have ever imagined."

"Brax has been worried."

"Tell him to stop. Jase is part of a huge family, and he knows more than most how life isn't fair and you just need to move on sometimes. That's how he feels about this."

"So, you're really moving to Jasper Creek?"

"Not until the baby is born. I want to be around my friends here when I give birth. We're thinking in the summer."

"What about you? How are you doing?" Bonnie asked. "You've been kidnapped twice."

"Brax talked me into counseling."

"Talked?"

"Forcefully encouraged," Jenny laughed ruefully. "It helped. There were other... older things I needed to work out, so it's helped a lot. I think I might even be a good mom one day."

"I'm sorry, did I just hear you say you thought you might be a good mom one day?" Brax asked as he handed her a glass of champagne.

Jenny blushed. "Maybe."

"This is my cue to exit," Bonnie said. She leaned over and kissed Jenny's cheek.

When she turned, she saw Brax staring down at her, his expression, intent.

"That's a pretty big step, Ms. Rivers. You believing in yourself that much."

Jenny nodded.

"You know, I had a lot of things planned for this evening. Us all dressed up nice, a band, there's dancing, we're in front of our friends. Seemed to me like a perfect setup."

"What are you talking about?" He was so confusing.

Brax plucked her champagne glass out of her hand and put it on one of the round tables and put his arm around her. "How about we go home and celebrate Jada and Gideon's nuptials alone? I can put on some music, and we can dance."

She saw the banked heat in his eyes, and her core clenched.

She nodded.

He took her hand and guided her outside to his truck. He lifted her into the passenger seat. On the way home her hands twisted in her lap. Tonight was her big night. She'd been planning for two weeks. She could do this.

Brax looked over at her.

"You holding up okay?"

"Yeah, why wouldn't I?"

"They're probably going to reach a settlement next week on your suit against New Era Cyber Tech. I noticed you were kind of twisted up lately."

"No, it wasn't that."

"Then you admit it's something."

"We're almost home, can we wait until then?" Jenny asked.

Brax held out his hand, and she grabbed it like a lifeline.

BRAX FELT like he could finally breathe now that Jenny was clutching his hand. He'd wanted her to go to counseling so she could feel better about herself. So she could work out her childhood demons and the kidnappings, but lately he'd worried that maybe she'd decided to kick him to the curb. Having her hold onto him like this eased an ache deep inside him.

"Stay there," he said when he pulled into his driveway. "I don't want you to mess up your dress or twist an ankle as you try to get out of the truck."

"Okay."

Brax came to the passenger seat and lifted her out, and they went into the house.

"Do you want a drink?" he asked.

"No, I want a clear head. Can you come sit down on the couch with me?"

Now he was worried again. But he nodded and did as she asked. When he sat down, and she stood in front of him, he drew in a deep breath and waited. He didn't have to wait long. She started to draw up the hem of her long bridesmaid dress until it came up to her thighs.

Fuck, she's wearing thigh high stockings.

"What are you doing?" he croaked out the question.

"Wait and see."

With a dainty wiggle, she lowered herself so that her knees bracketed his legs, and she was sitting on his lap, eye to eye. "I needed to get your full attention," she whispered.

"You've got it."

God, is this my voice? I sound like I swallowed a frog or something.

"I've told you many times how much I adore you. You know I adore you, right?"

He nodded. His gaze drifted down to her cleavage that somehow was sparkling tonight. Had she put some kind of sparkling makeup on?

She cupped his cheeks and lifted his head, then she bit his lower lip, hard.

"Concentrate, boy. I'm talking, here."

"I'm multi-tasking," he grinned.

"I need your total focus," she grinned back.

"Okay, you have it."

"Good. My speech isn't done. Now, I adore you. I

adore your body, your spirit, and the way you care and protect me."

Brax felt his heart melt, and he clutched her hips. "I love you, baby. I'll always be here for you."

"That's what I want you to know," she whispered. "I love you, too. No matter what comes at us in the future, whether we are together or not, you need to know I will love you forever. You need to know that my love for you is the best thing that has ever happened. You are the best thing that has ever happened in my life. You are a miracle."

He felt tears burning the backs of his eyes. "Damn, Jenny, when you go for it, you really go for it."

Her smile was beautiful.

"You got one thing wrong, though," he whispered.

She tilted her head to the side. "What?"

"Reach into my pants pocket."

She started to.

"Other pocket."

He saw her eyes go wide when she felt the jeweler's box.

"Open it," he commanded.

"No. Tell me what I got wrong first."

"You said whether we are together or not. Open the box so I can put on your ring. I want you to know that we will be together for always and beyond baby. For always and beyond."

Read the whole Omega Sky Series today
Her Selfless Warrior (Book #1)

ABOUT THE AUTHOR

Caitlyn O'Leary is a USA Bestselling Author, #1 Amazon Bestselling Author and a Golden Quill Recipient from Book Viral in 2015. Hampered with a mild form of dyslexia she began memorizing books at an early age until her grandmother, the English teacher, took the time to teach her to read -- then she never stopped. She began re-writing alternate endings for her Trixie Belden books into happily-ever-afters with Trixie's platonic friend Jim. When she was home with pneumonia at twelve, she read the entire set of World Book Encyclopedias -- a little more challenging to end those happily.

Caitlyn loves writing about Alpha males with strong heroines who keep the men on their toes. There is plenty of action, suspense and humor in her books. She is never shy about tackling some of today's tough and relevant issues.

In addition to being an award-winning author of romantic suspense novels, she is a devoted aunt, an avid reader, a former corporate executive for a Fortune 100 company, and totally in love with her husband of soon-to-be twenty years.

She recently moved back home to the Pacific Northwest from Southern California. She is so happy to see the seasons again; rain, rain and more rain. She has a large fan group on Facebook and through her e-mail list. Caitlyn is known for telling her "Caitlyn Factors", where she relates her little and big life's screw-ups. The list is long. She loves hearing and connecting with her fans on a daily basis.

Keep up with Caitlyn O'Leary:

Website: www.caitlynoleary.com
FB Reader Group: http://bit.ly/2NUZVjF
Email: caitlyn@caitlynoleary.com
Newsletter: http://bit.ly/1WIhRup

- facebook.com/Caitlyn-OLeary-Author-638771522866740
- x.com/CaitlynOLearyNA
- instagram.com/caitlynoleary_author
- amazon.com/author/caitlynoleary
- bookbub.com/authors/caitlyn-o-leary
- goodreads.com/CaitlynOLeary
- pinterest.com/caitlynoleary35

ALSO BY CAITLYN O'LEARY

PROTECTORS OF JASPER CREEK SERIES

His Wounded Heart (Book 1)

Her Hidden Smile (Book 2)

Their Stormy Reunion (Book 3)

Back To Our Beginning (Book 4)

OMEGA SKY SERIES

Her Selfless Warrior (Book #1)

Her Unflinching Warrior (Book #2)

Her Wild Warrior (Book #3)

Her Fearless Warrior (Book 4)

Her Defiant Warrior (Book 5)

Her Brave Warrior (Book 6)

Her Eternal Warrior (Book 7)

NIGHT STORM SERIES

Her Ruthless Protector (Book #1)

Her Tempting Protector (Book #2)

Her Chosen Protector (Book #3)

Her Intense Protector (Book #4)

Her Sensual Protector (Book #5)

Her Faithful Protector (Book #6)

Her Noble Protector (Book #7)

Her Righteous Protector (Book #8)

NIGHT STORM LEGACY SERIES

Lawson & Jill (Book 1)

BLACK DAWN SERIES

Her Steadfast Hero (Book #1)

Her Devoted Hero (Book #2)

Her Passionate Hero (Book #3)

Her Wicked Hero (Book #4)

Her Guarded Hero (Book #5)

Her Captivated Hero (Book #6)

Her Honorable Hero (Book #7)

Her Loving Hero (Book #8)

THE MIDNIGHT DELTA SERIES

Her Vigilant Seal (Book #1)

Her Loyal Seal (Book #2)

Her Adoring Seal (Book #3)

Sealed with a Kiss (Book #4)

Her Daring Seal (Book #5)

Her Fierce Seal (Book #6)

A Seals Vigilant Heart (Book #7)

Her Dominant Seal (Book #8)

Her Relentless Seal (Book #9)

Her Treasured Seal (Book #10)

Her Unbroken Seal (Book #11)

THE LONG ROAD HOME

Defending Home

Home Again

FATE HARBOR

Trusting Chance

Protecting Olivia

Isabella's Submission

Claiming Kara

Cherishing Brianna

SILVER SEALS

Seal At Sunrise

SHADOWS ALLIANCE SERIES

Declan

Made in the USA
Las Vegas, NV
13 December 2024

14054544R00177